The Cagliostro Chronicles

By Ralph L. Angelo Jr.

The
Cagliostro Chronicles
By
Ralph L. Angelo, Jr.
Cover by Gustav Barta
Edited by Deborah Richardson
Of DRE&MS
Published by Cosmic Comet Publishing
Copyright 2013 By Ralph L. Angelo, Jr.

Dedicated to the kids in my life, Tara, Sammy, Madeline and Nicholas! You guys all rock! Love ya! Uncle Ralph.

Table of Contents

Chapter One

"3, 2, 1…IGNITION!"

The great ship shook, vibrating so heavily those sitting within its command deck area held on for dear life as their vision blurred. Mark Johnson sat in the Captain's chair and cursed inwardly, shaking his head he said "Shut it down."

"It's not supposed to do that, is it?" A stocky man sitting in a plush chair behind the pilot's display turned in his seat, and said to Mark.

"No Danny, It's not." Johnson replied as he slumped back in his seat, annoyance written all over his face.

Dan Sledge sighed as he stood up. "Relax Mark; I'll get right on it. The issue has gotta be with the gyroscopic navigation and balance system."

"All right Danny. Keep me informed. I'll be down to the engineering bay as soon as possible."

Dan Sledge nodded and walked away, toward the elevator on the left side of the command deck, and after entering the single entrant wide elevator sideways due to the width of his shoulders, disappeared. He was a very powerfully built man. At six feet tall he looked far larger than he actually was, because he had a huge amount of muscle packed on him. That was due to his heritage as a member of the famed Jupiter colony where he was born. He had been born in a floating city high above Jupiter that was placed there as a gas mine. His lineage had been genetically altered to allow for the incredibly increased gravity of the place. Not only was the denser musculature needed to simply walk around in such a high gravity environment, but it aided in moving equipment that weighed many tons more than it would on earth. Most machinery would crumble under its own weight in such a place. But people like Dan, genetically engineered to be super-humanly strong took all the guess work out of gas mining above Jupiter.

His strength was significantly more than a normal earthborn man's. He could lift many tons easily, due to his unique musculature, but he had the heart of a teddy bear.

Next to his console a gorgeous blonde sat and swiveled her seat until it was facing Mark Johnson's. She smiled warmly and offered, "It'll be all right Mark. Danny'll straighten it out."

Mark Johnson nodded as he stood up from his command chair. He was a good looking man with medium length brown hair. He stood about six foot two and weighed in the neighborhood of two hundred pounds. Not thin, not heavy. He had suppleness to his movements that some compared to a panther. "You're right Ariel, I know you are, but I have to worry about this stuff. It's my name out there." He waved towards the outside of the ship and the hangers in the distance.

Ariel nodded, "I understand Mark, but try to relax anyway. This will all work out. You know that." Her wavy blonde hair fell between her shoulders as she turned her chair and returned to her position at her monitoring station. Ariel O'Conner was drop dead gorgeous. She stood five feet seven inches tall and had perfect looks, like a Goddess. But she had something else going for her too. She was a telepath. A very powerful telepath. All of Mark Johnson's command crew were special people. Ariel was his communications or 'comm' officer, and she was also his girlfriend.

Mark nodded in agreement then turned his head toward a man sitting at the next console over from Ariel, "Eddie, how are the weapon diagnostics going? Tell me something good, Mr. DiGenovese." Sitting across from Ariel's station was Eddie DiGenovese. Eddie was a dark haired man about five foot nine inches tall, and around a solid one hundred and eighty pounds. His boyish good looks and quick smile melted many a ladies hearts, but that wasn't all Eddie melted. When he fired the ships weapons, or his hand blaster with pinpoint accuracy he could melt out a key hole at half a mile. His expertise had yet to meet its match. "Well, boss, I gotta tell you, it's all good here so far. I think the weapons banks are fine. You do good work." Eddie grinned.

Mark nodded and turned toward the last member of his command crew. "Red, anything to report? Are we okay? Or did we wake the enemy?"

The fifth member of the crew was the security officer or sergeant at arms. He stood six foot four and was a rock solid two hundred twenty pounds of muscle. His red hair and freckled face belied his no-nonsense temperament. He was a bruiser, trained in many different fighting styles. To this day, James "Red" Robinski worked out two hours every day. One hour building muscle, another hour practicing fighting techniques. He always had a dour expression on his pale face, and was not known to be the happiest of persons. But most importantly he was unmatched at his job, and he was completely and absolutely loyal to Mark Johnson. As were all in his security detail. "Mark, everything is fine. All security details have checked in, but it looks like we're going to have some company in the next few minutes. I'm picking up hover tank movements in quadrant four, aimed directly at us and closing fast."

"The general?" Ariel asked Mark.

"I have to assume. I mean who else could it be?" He turned to her, and then to all the command crew, looking over the expectant faces of everyone watching him, "I'm getting tired of these impromptu visits."

"Tell him that." Ariel urged.

"Won't matter Ari. There's more going on here than you know right now, but I promise I'll explain it to all of you soon, once we get off planet."

Ariel walked up to Mark who was staring out the big view screen before the command crew. Right now it showed where the ship was 'parked' in the middle of nowhere, meaning deep within the Arizona desert, and the Johnson Space and Aeronautical Corporation test facilities.

"Mark, relax. This will happen. The Cagliostro will fly." Ariel began, her smooth voice softly toying with his ears.

"I know Ariel. But I need to get it space borne in the next few days. We have to get off planet sooner than later."

"Why?"

"Because of him." he jerked his thumb towards the view screen "I'll fill you in later, all of you. This is big, and right now I have to deal with our company."

Ariel turned and looked out the view screen, then cursed softly under her breath. "Do you want me to come with you?"

"No Ari. I'll handle the General."

Outside, now facing the great ship Cagliostro were a half dozen powerful hover tanks as well as an old style gasoline powered jeep, where a cigar chewing, army General stood up and looked over the top of the windshield. He was a heavy set man about six feet one inches tall. His gray mustache quivered on his lip as he beheld the Cagliostro for the first time. He whipped off his sunglasses and huffed and puffed on his cigar before jumping off the jeep, fists clenched, he stomped determinedly towards the Cagliostro itself.

"Johnson!" He roared. "I know you hear me Johnson! Get out here! You and I need to talk, and talk now."

Mark sighed, shook his head and walked toward the elevator on the right side of the command deck.

'Do you want me to at least stay mind linked with you?' Ariel spoke within the confines of both their minds.

'Up to you hon,' Johnson replied in the same manner, "Though I have a feeling my conversation with the General is about to become a bit...colorful."

'Okay, I'll cut the link. If you need me holler, I'll hear that.'

'Sure thing, babe.'

Ariel severed their link while Mark exited the command deck and a moment later was outside the Cagliostro and walking toward the General.

"What are you doing here, General?"

"I came to see what all the ruckus was that I had just heard about."

"And just how'd you hear about my engine test so quickly, General?"

The older man pointed towards space with the hand holding his cigar. "We have these new-fangled things you might have heard of, they're called satellites."

"So you *are* watching me." Mark replied, with anger coloring his voice now.

"Of course we're watching you, Johnson. It's 2089, everyone is watching everyone. You promised the United States military your faster than light magnetic drive. We mean to watch over our investment."

"There is no investment, General, not yet. I funded this faster than light drive out of my own pocket, as you well know. I have no problem selling it to my nation after I test it, but I decide when and if it's ready to be put into production. Not you, or anyone else." He turned to stare at the gleaming space ship towering above him.

"No one is trying to step on your toes son; we just want to make sure you have the best interests of your country at heart. Look, you know you are about to make history with this new ship of yours. Mankind has never flown through space faster than light before. Isn't it best to have the United States military making that great achievement? It's something for the history books, son. Like Washington crossing the Potomac, or the Wright Brothers first flight. Think like a patriot son. You are a patriot, aren't you?"

Johnson turned and faced the General with anger playing at the corners of his mouth. "General, you pulled up here on to my property with six, count 'em six of the hover tanks I designed, built and sold to the government. My patriotism is unmatched by anyone in Washington or anywhere else for that matter. Secondly, all the greatest moments in mankind's history have come from individual engineers, scientists and free thinkers, NOT the government, which can't even run itself because of all its largesse. Now you go back to your superiors and tell them that I will gladly sell them the designs for not only my magno-disc engine design, but the starships that go with them, when I decide it is safe to put them into production. Not before. No soldier will be put at risk because of me. Good day General."

Johnson turned and walked away before the General could say another word.

Two minutes later he was back on the command deck, sitting in his plush Captains chair staring at the six hover tanks which were just now powering up and floating away, The jeep remained a moment longer with the old man standing within it and staring at the magnificent ship before finally sitting down and barking orders at his driver to get them out of there. External microphones picked up the General's order.

"This ship has to be in space tomorrow." Johnson commented loudly enough for everyone who remained on the command deck to hear him.

Mark stood and silently returned to the elevator, descending to the engineering bay. The magnetic elevators were a marvel. Not only did they move up and down, but side to side as well. Now after dropping to the fifth level out of the ten on the ship, the magnetic elevator, or 'maglovator', whisked him toward the tail of the ship, stopping in the ships center, where the doors slid open.

Dan Sledge raised his head at Marks arrival and nodded, smiling.

"Any luck, Danny?"

"I'm on the right track boss-man. Magno-disc balance system was a few ticks off. It's gonna take me a while to get 'em re-aligned."

"How long?" Mark asked stoically.

"Mebbe six hours or so."

"Get it finished in two, Dan. I need to get us into space ASAP."

"Why? What's up? Are we in trouble?"

"Maybe. I don't like the way General Abruzzi was carrying on out there. I don't trust him. I have a bad feeling he's going to try some legal wrangling to take the ship away from me."

"I'll be done here as fast as possible."

"I'm counting on it Dan. If you need an extra set of hands down here, let me know. I designed most of this system anyway."

"Naaah, you go back up top boss. You've got enough on yer mind. Let me an' the boys down here handle this."

Johnson nodded stoically, "All right Danny, I won't stand around hovering over your shoulder. If you need me, call."

Before leaving Mark walked around the engineering bay and stopped at a schematic of the ship on a display. Its smooth rounded lines from the side did not show the entire shape of the ship, only a side view. The dimensions were written next to the ships image on the screen before him.

They were one thousand feet long, two hundred and fifty feet high (body height, not from the ground, add another fifty feet for take-off and landing apparatus that retracted and hid in the belly of the ship once it was underway.), and six hundred feet wide. Mark tapped the screen and a view from above the ship now filled the screen. This view showed an almost exact depiction of a Manta Ray with a few additions. Instead of just the center tail of the real fish, there were two additional tail-like trailing edges at each side of the rear of the ship, for a total of three tail-like protuberances. Ten decks made up the ship, with fifty foot armored sections top and bottom before you even reached a deck. It was a juggernaut for its size. All it had to do was get off the ground.

"Danny, really, what can I do to help?"

Sledge stood up and looked at his boss and friend, then smiled slightly, "Mark, go back upstairs. Seriously, I got this."

Mark nodded and walked off towards the deck hallway. The doors hissed open as he approached and sighed close behind him. He walked down the empty hallway and smiled as he ran his fingers across the spotless, gleaming white wall.

Entering the Maglovator, Johnson punched a few buttons and exited back upon the command deck a moment later. He looked about him one more time, then spoke "Hey everyone, listen up. Take an hour. Go to your quarters aboard ship. Take a shower and put on your uniforms, relax a little bit, but be ready to go at a moment's notice. I have a feeling we may be heading into space very soon, possibly within the hour. So don't fall asleep on me. I need you all.

Just make sure you put the new uniforms on. I want everyone wearing them when we take off. Thanks. Now go on. Get out of here." He concluded.

The rest of the command deck personal, the non-essential staff all headed to the dual maglovators talking amongst themselves.

The command deck was almost empty now as Mark sat back in his chair and looked out the view screen.

"Are you okay?"

Mark turned around and saw Ariel standing behind him, arms crossed, leaning against the wall by the maglovator. She walked towards him and sat in his lap. "Are you okay?" She repeated.

"So far. Abruzzi is going to try to take the 'Cag', I can feel it. We have to get her out of here as soon as possible. I will not lose control of this ship and the design work that went into her."

"Mark, what's the difference if they buy her from you or not?"

"Ari, this is *my* ship. I didn't design this one for NASA or the government or anyone else. I built her with my money exclusively. There was no contract signed for anything on this ship. Yes, I guaranteed the new faster than light magno-disc propulsion system for sale to them, but that's only going to happen after we run our own test flights. Also, like I said, this is my ship. It's not under anyone else's rules or jurisdictions. I run this baby. Everyone on this ship is on my payroll and they are the most trusted of employees."

Ariel shook her head "Sometimes I really do think that you are nuts." She replied as she got up out of his lap and walked behind her chair.

He walked over to her and grabbed her arms lightly while staring her in the eyes. "Look Ari, you have to trust me on this one. There's more going on here then I can talk about right here and now. You're going to have to let me run with this. I'll fill you in as soon as I'm able to. When it's safe for you and everyone aboard this tub."

She smiled whimsically at him, "A minute ago this was your baby, now it's a tub?"

He leaned forward and kissed her, then pulled back. "YOU'RE my baby. This IS just a tub compared to you. But it's a tub I'm passionate about. This ship is going to be special."

Ariel smiled at him, "It already is, with you in control of things."

Mark laughed"You are one cool chick."

"Make sure you remember that, rocket scientist." She smiled over her shoulder, and walked away.

"Ariel," he called after her, "Go put your uniform on, will you please?"

"Wanna help me big boy?" She winked at him playfully.

"Any other time you couldn't keep me away, but for right now I'll have to take a rain check."

Ariel pouted a moment, then left the command deck and headed to her own quarters.

A moment later Johnson left the now empty command deck and headed to his quarters. He exited forty-five minutes later wearing his own uniform. It was a one piece semi-shiny light-blue and silver suit. It was temperature controlled by an interwoven technology within the fabric, as well as being decidedly sturdy. It would resist most bullets as well as lasers and pulsed weaponry to a certain point. It still wouldn't feel good being hit by any of those, though. But the wearer wouldn't be killed, at least not the majority of the time.

Mark Johnson exited the maglovator and re-entered the command deck. He looked around the command deck and saw everyone was wearing their uniforms. The place was alive. Sounds were emanating from just about everywhere as decks were checking in with Ariel.

Mark sat down in his command chair and looked around smiling. On the right side of his chair, a yellow light was blinking. He tapped it and immediately Dan Sledge's voice filled the area around him. "I found it boss-man. We should be good to go."

"Good work Danny, now get your butt back up here, I'm going to begin launch procedures."

Mark noticed every head turn to look at him when he finished talking to Sledge.

"Patch me through to the rest of the ship, Ariel."

She nodded and clicked a virtual button.

"This is Mark Johnson." His voice reverberated throughout the ship, "We are about to go into space, but I have to warn you all, this is going to be more than a test flight. There's a good chance we will be gone for several weeks. If any of you want to stay on Earth due to family or any other reasons, I understand. I'm just going to ask you to exit the ship as soon as possible. We're getting ready to lift off and I do not foresee us being on the ground for more than another twenty minutes. Once the doors shut, they are shut and you will be with us for the long haul."

Some throughout the ship looked nervous, some excited, but they all knew what was about to happen. History was about to be made.

Chapter Two

"Engines starting." The burly engineer proclaimed from his seat on the command deck.

This time there was nothing out of the ordinary. There were no more filling loosening vibrations as the crew had first experienced, no loud noises that froze the hearts of weaker men. Just a very low and slight hum that soon disappeared completely.

Johnson smiled, "Sounds good, Dan."

"Want me to take her up?" The big engineer replied.

"Not this time Danny. I've got it." Mark tapped a button on the arm display of his chair and instantly a holographic pilot's display and controls appeared before him. He touched a few of the holographic controls and with small puffs of sand; the ship gently rose majestically from the desert floor.

Slowly at first, then faster as its speed doubled, tripled and then quadrupled within a few scant seconds, the ship rose out of the Arizona desert and pointed its majestic body skyward.

"Ten seconds till we break atmosphere" Sledge reported with a big grin on his face.

A light beeped on Ariel's display, she turned towards Johnson. "That's The General. He wants to know where we're going and why wasn't he informed the ship was space worthy?"

"Tell him we'll talk after our rundown flight."

She paused a moment, then, "He disconnected me. I don't remember him being this hard headed."

"Ignore him; we're in space right… about… NOW!" Johnson finished with a smile as the big manta ray shaped ship broke the final vestiges of atmosphere and left Earth's last remnants behind.

"Mr. Sledge, the controls are yours." A beaming Mark Johnson proclaimed.

"Thank you sir." Dan Sledge replied with a smile of his own, as his controls took over when Mark's shut down.

A heartbeat later a beeping sound and a corresponding blinking light appeared on Sledge's display.

"Hey Boss-man, we got company." Mark was out of his seat and standing next to Dan instantly.

"What is it?"

Sledge waited an instant as the verification software compared long range scans, then furrowed his brow as he replied, "Uh Mark, that's a 'Goliath' class star cruiser. I just received verification; it's the 'War-Hammer'." Sledge swiveled in his chair to face Mark.

"Would Abruzzi send a war ship after us?" Ariel asked in surprise.

"It looks he already did." Mark replied, as he sat back in his seat. "Eddie just in case, have the solar cannons online. I don't want to fire on a US Navy space ship, but I'm going to take this ship out of here whether General Abruzzi likes it or not."

"You do realize if we disobey a direct order from that ship we will automatically be performing an act of treason, right?" Eddie asked.

"Well, under normal circumstances, yes Eddie. But these are not normal circumstances. You're all going to have to trust me on this."

As he finished speaking the ship suddenly shuddered for an instant, as a flash of light played across the view screen.

"They just fired on us." Red shouted from his security console.

"Yeah, we got that." Eddie replied over the alert klaxons that were now going off.

"Red, kill that thing." Johnson ordered, and the klaxon went silent.

"The War-Hammer is hailing us." Ariel stated flatly.

"Let's see what they have to say."

Ariel nodded as the view screen turned to an image of the gray haired Captain of the War-Hammer, "This is Captain O'Neal of the USS War-Hammer. You are ordered to return from whence you launched and await General Abruzzi from there. Am I understood?"

Mark leaned forward in his seat and replied, "I'm sorry Captain O'Neal, but this is a private ship and is free to do as I deem necessary. We are under no military jurisdiction whatsoever. Give the General my regards, and you, yourself, have a nice day." As he finished he slashed across his throat with his first two fingers on his left hand while looking at Ariel. She immediately killed the connection.

"Danny get us away from that ship, then power up the magno-discs to one hundred percent and get us out of here."

"Already on it, boss-man." Sledge replied.

"Incoming!" Shouted Red.

A shockingly bright blast enveloped the ship's command deck for an instant and then passed as the Cagliostro shuddered from within.

"How's integrity?" Johnson asked Sledge.

"Hull integrity is perfect. That hull armor you insisted on is holding up fine as of now."

"Now you know why I insisted on fifty feet of it both top and bottom of the ship."

"Yeah I do." Sledge shook his head in the affirmative.

"Good, now get the magnetic defense shielding up."

Sledge turned back to his console and pressed a button, immediately a blue glow wrapped around the ship, deflecting enemy fire easily.

"NOW we're protected." Red added.

"Yes, we are. Pilot, it's time to earn your pay. Get us out of here." Mark commanded.

Dan Sledge smiled, "With pleasure, Boss." He ran his fingers up the clear touch screen and the ships engines began to hum strongly.

"We got more trouble." Red barked, "Another ship incoming on an immediate approach vector. They're trying to wedge us between them." He turned when finished.

"What is it?" Mark questioned.

"Rapier class fast attack cruiser." Red replied.

"Okay let's rock and roll. Bring us in tight to the 'War-Hammer', I want us hugging its skin, then it's time to go faster than light. Hit it Dan."

Sledge nodded and brought the engines to full power, as energy blasts were now aimed directly at them and splattering on their shields, rocking the ship as it started to accelerate.

"How are the shields holding?"

"They're taking a beating from both ships out there. They're down to seventy-five percent. The way those things are pounding at us, we won't last much longer."

"Won't need any longer." Sledge grunted as the Cagliostro rocketed along the side of the big War-Hammer. Sliding past it and between the closing Rapier class ship. "Hold onto your stomachs, cause here we go!"

A sudden surge of acceleration pushed everyone back into their seats, and after an instant they were gone!

On the view screen before their stunned eyes the command staff watched in awe as stars and planets were left behind in a ghost-like state. Seemingly nothing more than an afterimage.

"Whoa." Eddie DiGenovese whispered in awe.

"Whoa is right Eddie. We are now the first humans to officially break the light speed barrier. Welcome to history."

"No wonder Abruzzi wanted this for the military first." Ariel commented.

Mark didn't say anything, keeping his council to himself.

"Okay so when do I turn this baby around?" Sledge asked.

"You don't. I'm going to punch in some coordinates. That is where we're going." Mark replied as he called forth the virtual instrumentation in front of his Captains chair once again, and tapped a few buttons.

Dan turned towards him when he read the coordinates, his face screwed up quizzically. "This is a pretty damned far trip, you know that right?"

"Yes, I do, Dan. Just get us there."

Dan shook his head to one side, then murmured "Glad I packed some extra socks."

Mark smiled as Ariel looked at him strangely once before turning back to her console.

"All right Dan, Eddie, Ariel and Red, meet me in the conference room in five. Ari, call the secondary crew to the command deck while we're there." Mark stood up and headed towards the maglovator.

***

"What's going on here?" Red Robinski asked. "Why are we suddenly flying further into space then man has ever gone which we already have crossed that threshold by the way, and going to some mysterious coordinates that you happened to have in hand the minute we clear Earth's gravity well?" Red was agitated, as he always seemed to be.

Johnson smiled as he leaned back in his chair at the briefing table within the command room. "That's why I like having you around Red, you keep me honest."

Robinski looked at him through slit eyes, "What's that supposed to mean? What are you holding back from us?"

"Look guys, you are right, I have been holding something back from you all. But this is big, really big actually. Like world changing big. I wanted to tell you earlier, heck I tried earlier today and then the general showed up and it had to wait."

The four of them focused on him seriously at this point. Johnson sighed and then began, "Last week I had a meeting with the President, and it wasn't the first one."

"What about?" Dan asked slowly.

"This is deep, my friends. I tried explaining this earlier before the General interrupted us. There's a traitor within the government, a mole. This is the part you're not going to believe, it's an alien. They know that for a fact. There's an alien race targeting the United States government and its space program."

"Why?" Red asked, with a furrowed brow.

"Because they do not want us to perfect interstellar flight. Which I don't have to remind you, *we* just did."

"Again, why the interest in us?"

"The President thinks it's because we are dangerous. As a race we know one thing very well. That's how to blow things up, and kill the enemy. The President believes that someone is trying to keep us sequestered in our corner of the galaxy so fifty or a hundred years from now we won't be challenging anyone for galactic supremacy."

"Why would they think we would do that?" Ariel asked, obviously perplexed.

"The answer's obvious," Red replied, "We're conquerors. As a race we climb the highest mountain, swim the deepest ocean, etc. We explore until we run out of things to find in any given area and then we move on to a new area and start over."

"That's right Red. That was pretty much the Presidents assumption as well. He asked me to undertake this journey, to head up this investigation, and to do it surreptitiously. That's why us and not the military."

"Okay, but what about our vaunted spy organizations? Why couldn't they do it?"

"In what ship? This is the only 'Faster than Light' or 'FTL' ship on Earth. We have a huge space armada, but none have ever broken the light barrier. The Cagliostro is the fastest ship known to man. It's also one tough sucker as well. Between our shielding system, which withstood an onslaught from two powerful fleet war ships only a few hours ago, and our deck armor, we are virtually untouchable. At least for a while."

"So does he have any idea who the spy is?" Eddie asked.

"No. He's not sure. But he has a few suspicions."

"So where'd these mysterious coordinates come from?"

"They managed to track a signal that was bouncing off a few of our satellites before being received somewhere in D.C. It was filtered and splashed about so that it had no real recipient that could be found. It hit a wide range of space, before it was received by its mysterious recipient. All we know is it came from the coordinates we're going to."

"Which is not the best news I've heard all day." Eddie replied.

"How so?" Dan asked.

"Real Simple, Danny-boy, we have no idea what we are heading into. At all. This could be either a military base, a planet of space-pirates, which by the way, the concept of does not thrill me in the least. A planet of a warrior race, God only knows what else? We are really flying blind right now. We're heading into trouble."

"And that Eddie," Mark began, "Is why we have to be prepared for all eventualities. Look team, we're going to be in FTL for at least a week until we find this signal's origin point. Everyone here has to be sharp. We're going to be running some training scenarios over the next week. We have to be at our best, because not only am I, but the whole world as well is relying on us. We may be the Earths first, last, and best line of defense."

"So everything is riding on us." Red finished.

"You could say that, Red. Look, the bottom line is that someone out there set their sights on Earth for whatever reason, and we have to find out why and what for."

"Do you think there's an imposter involved?" Ariel asked, "You know what I mean, someone who was planted taking the place of someone high up in the government?"

"I think that's a definite possibility, Ariel. I even have a few suspicions as to who it may be."

"Care to share that information?" Red asked as he clasped his fists and leaned forward on the table.

Mark turned toward him before speaking, "No. I'm not going to. It's best if only I know who is suspected and who is above suspicion."

"Wassamatter? Don't trust us Mark?" Eddie asked, with a crooked grin.

"It's not that at all, Eddie, and you know the answer to that already. The reason is simple, the less people who know who is under suspicion the less that can inadvertently give that information away."

"Like if one of us gets captured and tortured or something?" Dan Sledge asked.

"Precisely, Dan. If they come for one of us let it be me. Not any of you."

"Very heroic Mister, but that's a load and you know it." Ariel barked angrily.

Johnson sighed and grabbed her hand, "No Ari, it's not. It's the truth. I need all of you to be able to do your jobs and I need to know you can all get me out of whatever hell hole they take me to in case I do get captured."

"So what about these aliens? Do we know anything about them? How long have they been watching us?" Eddie queried, "I mean, up until now, all of Earth's fleet has been stuck exploring around the solar system. Taking off for years at a time. Sure the ships have been getting faster every year, but they still take literally years to get somewhere. Your magno-disc technology is changing all that, and since this morning it's no longer even a theory. It's pure fact. Man has jumped to the head of the class."

"That's exactly what we theorize they are frightened of, whoever the mysterious 'they' are, that is. Now there's suddenly competition, and it's all coming from Earth."

"But that's the part I don't get," Eddie interjects, "Competition for what?"

"Eddie, it could be anything. Manufacturing ability, mining, science breakthroughs, though personally I can't see them being behind us on that one. It could even be weapons design. Bottom line is we just do not know, but we are going to find out. "

***

Days passed quietly enough as the Cagliostro continued on through deep space. Its magno-disc engines purring lightly as the ship soared on at speeds that only days earlier were inconceivable to man.

The command crew continued to train diligently every day for whatever might cross their paths. Still, there was an air of trepidation throughout everyone on board. Mark had held a conference with the entire crew that first evening telling them they were on a mission for the government,

23

which was the truth anyway, and that they would be away from home for a few weeks. Subspace messages were sent to loved ones by the entire crew.

Daily, crew members lined up by fore and aft view screens, watching the stars go by in that elongated hyper-light way they now realized stars actually did look like when you were partially phased between dimensions, as the Cagliostro's magno-disc faster than light technology actually did. Not only was this an indescribable first time experience for everyone on board, it was an incredible visual one as well. Everything was running smoothly.

Until the fourth day.

Red looked up from his display and then back down at it, immediately punching it up on the main view screen. "You better look at this Mark."

Johnson leaned forward slightly in his chair on the 'D' shaped command deck "Looks like we have company. Better move us to yellow status."

Red nodded and immediately yellow lights spun at each corner of the command deck as well as throughout the ship and for ten seconds an alert tone pinged on every deck.

Behind the Cagliostro three blips were seen gaining on them through the faster than light conduit, or hyper-warp tunnel.

"Dan, can we increase speed?"

"Uh, yeah, Mark, we're just under halfway to full speed, as you know anyway, but yes, we have a ways to go."

"Just checking, big guy. Bring her up two more notches and let's see if they match."

Sledge complied as the ship eased forward faster, immediately leaving the three shapeless blips behind them completely.

For a moment.

But then…

"They're back, Boss." Red informed them all.

"Let's try this again, Dan, two more notches up to hyper-warp eight. Sledge thumbed his controls and the ship imperceptibly leapt ahead again leaving its mysterious pursuers behind, yet once more.

Minutes passed as silence coated the interior of the command deck heavily.

Finally Mark broke the overwhelming pall, "Well?"

"Nothing Boss. They disappeared." Red replied.

"To be honest, I'm kind of finding it hard to believe they couldn't keep up with us. I mean this is our first time doing this. I would think they'd be able to fly rings around us and leave us sucking their interstellar exhaust." Sledge offered.

"You would think so, right?" Mark replied with a smile.

"So what now?" Eddie asked.

"Now we continue to scan as far in front and behind the ship as possible. I also think we should maintain this speed at least another six hours to really put some distance between those ships and us, if that is what we are doing." Mark commented.

"Having doubts? Dan asked.

"As you said Danny, they should be able to catch us and leave us behind, easily. At least I would think so. Unless I'm better than I believe."

"Is such a thing even possible?" Ariel asked almost under her breath, with a smirk.

Mark shot her a glance with a smirk of his own, then continued talking to the rest of the crew. "We don't even know what that was. Those three blips could have been personal ships for all we know out for a buzz around the galaxy."

"What? Like outer space joy riders?" Eddie asked, as he furrowed his brow questioningly.

"Yes, why not? We don't know what goes on out here. It literally could have been anything. We are the new kids in the sandbox. We don't know the rules of the game yet."

"Uh, Mark," Red interjected, "I don't think this is a game, they're back."

Suddenly the ship rocked as a triplicate of energy blasts struck its rear hull from the just returned three vessels.

"Okay, let's see what we have here, people. Eddie power up aft solar cannons and fire on my mark. Keep power down to forty percent for now. I don't want to disintegrate these guys. Dan maintain speed and heading until I say otherwise, Red, shields at full power. Let's see what we've got."

"Nothing like a little trial by fire to get the blood flowing." Red sneered, then continued, "They're firing on us again." Red added.

"Okay enough of that Eddie, return fire."

"Aye, Aye Cap'n." Eddie replied as he hit a virtual button atop his console.

Behind the big ship the three tail-like appendages glowed momentarily and then spit solar fire from their tips. Each ship was engulfed by the energy beams and immediately broke off pursuit, stopping dead in their tracks at awkward angles.

"What do we do now, Mark?" Sledge asked.

"Leave them. We don't know if they are playing dead or not. Those blasts were only forty percent power. Truthfully if we had fired those on the War-Hammer it would have barely registered it."

"Those were small craft though, Mark. Maybe there were one or two people aboard each." Red replied. "I'm sure we did far more damage on those little attack fliers then we could have on something like the War-Hammer."

"Listen people, we don't know the rules out here. This could be the Wild West for all we know. Those ships attacked us. We are going to continue on. They dropped out of hyper-warp far behind us already. I'm not going back. They were hostile; we have a mission to complete, period. Maintain course and speed, Dan."

"Will do, Boss." Dan replied as the ship continued to cut majestically through space.

Chapter Three

"We cut off another day by increasing our speed when we were attacked."

"I assumed as much, Dan. When we near our destination I want to slow this ship down outside the solar system we'll be visiting. In fact, I want to enter that solar system at sub light and start long range scans as soon as we're able. Look for any moons that will shield us from prying eyes, or dead planets we can maintain an orbit behind."

"So you want to get a look-see first?" Ariel asked.

"Yes I do, Ari. This is all new to us and we are literally out of reach as far as any help is concerned. I want a full diagnostic on this ship as soon as we reach somewhere secluded."

Dan Sledge turned towards his Captain, "Boss, everything is good. The ship's humming like a bird. We're good to go."

"Nevertheless Danny, I want it all gone over. Especially engine dynamics, structural integrity and, most especially, weapons and shields. If we have to pull out of there at a moment's notice I want to make sure everything is taken into account. No one will be coming to rescue us if things go badly."

"Uhh, Mark?" Ariel interrupted, "You better look at this." She punched a few buttons on her console and the view screen shimmered revealing a ship heading directly towards them also at hyper-warp speed.

"How long till we intercept it, or it intercepts us actually?" Mark asked icily.

"At the rate we are both traveling, ten more minutes. It knows we're here too. We were just scanned."

"No doubt it's coming to meet us. This is probably friends of whoever was in those three ships we disabled."

"I think that's a safe bet, Mark." Red replied as he went over the readouts before him, "This thing is huge too. It's almost a mile long, and loaded with weapons. I'm getting all kinds of readings, and they do have weapons powered up as of now, shields too. They're looking for a fight."

"If they want a fight, I have to assume they know exactly who we are as well."

"Are you going to try to talk to them?"

Johnson smiled, "I'll make the effort, Ariel, but I'll bet you lunch it's a waste of time."

She returned the smile and activated the controls on her console, then nodded to him. "This is Mark Johnson of the USS Cagliostro. We send peaceful greetings and look forward to talking to you. Please respond."

Silence reigned aboard the command deck as both ships hurtled towards each other. Mark looked at the view screen first, then over to Ariel, "Resend that message one more time. I'm not going to waste my breath repeating myself."

Ariel nodded and resent the message. The response was immediate this time and telling, as energy beams raked across the Cagliostro's hull, setting off emergency klaxons immediately.

"Mark!" Shouted Red instantly, "That thing just dropped our shields and power levels by thirty five percent. More importantly it dropped us from hyper-warp to normal space."

Mark leaped from his seat and hovered over Red's control panel. "They drained our energy stores? How is that even possible?"

"You're the engineer, boss, you tell me?" Red answered.

"Dan, evasive maneuvers," Mark shouted, "don't let them hit us again. Prepare to return fire at will. FIRE!"

Sledge turned the smooth lined ship in a tight arc, and flipped it over, avoiding two streams of energy that blasted space near enough to the ship to elicit rumbling vibrations throughout it.

Eddie began firing the ships solar cannons repeatedly, scoring direct hits multiple times across the hull of the much larger ship.

"Any damage?" Mark asked.

"Minor, boss. Nothing to speak of."

As they spoke the larger ship fired again and this time they struck pay dirt, as their energy weapons seemingly exploded across the Cag's shields and hull, sending the ship careening lopsidedly through space.

"Red!" Johnson shouted as emergency lights blinked across every console, and sirens blared.

"Shields and power down to twenty five percent."

"Okay, time to try something different and unorthodox. On my order, fire two non-nuclear high yield missiles at that things engines, but first sweep the hull with the cannons. After the cannon sweep, activate the magno-disc powered tractor beam and pull the thing off its trajectory. Let's see if we can shake them up."

Eddie looked at Mark for an instant, incredulously, and then a smile began to form on his lips as he turned back towards his controls. Red nodded seriously at Mark as he turned back towards his control panel, as well.

"You're up first, Eddie. Red, as soon as the solar cannons rake its hull, grab it with the tractor beam, and shake it hard. Eddie let those missiles fly the instant the tractor beam is fired."

Eddie nodded and fired the solar cannons. The twin energy beams leapt from the Cagliostro's bow, raking across the huge ship before them. An instant after they finished their sweep the tractor beam was engaged and immediately the enemy vessel seemed to buck and shake in space.

"I can't hold this long Eddie, There's strain on every system already." Red shouted.

"Already ahead of ya, big guy." Eddie DiGenovese replied, as he fired the missiles. They snaked through space unerringly on target, and then slammed into the larger ships engines, huge explosions engulfed both engines, with flames spouting all about the ship.

"Their shields are down!" Red growled

"NOW Eddie, FIRE!" Mark ordered.

Instantly Eddie fired the cannons again and again, hammering at the area already weakened by the missile strike. The enemy ship shuddered once, and then seemed to fall over to one side. It lay there dead in space, smoke and sparks peeled into the airless void from several spots along its huge frame.

"Are we able to go to hyper-warp?" Mark asked quickly.

"Yes." Sledge replied.

"GO!"

The ship leaped forward again, disappearing into hyper-warp.

"Forget what I said earlier, I want a status report on this entire ship *before* we arrive at that target solar system." Mark barked tensely. Then he stood up and exited the command deck. An instant later Ariel followed him out into the maglovator.

"What are you doing?" She asked tensely.

"What do you think?" He replied just as anxiously. "I *had* to get out of there for a few minutes. That was intense! Really intense. Wow! A real space fight and we won!" He exclaimed enthusiastically as he grabbed Ariel and gripped her by her arms, shaking her as he spoke.

"What is wrong with you? We all could have died a few minutes ago. Get it together." She replied angrily.

"I am together. I'm celebrating. This was a huge test for us all, and we not only passed, we passed with flying colors. This ship, all of us, we did great."

She sighed, then looked at him shaking her head, "What is the matter with you? Have you lost your mind? We could be in big trouble out here. Yes, we won one big outer space dogfight, but that's it. Plus we took some damage. Who knows when the ship will be back in fighting trim? What has gotten into you?"

"This is exhilarating, all of this. Don't you realize we're doing what no human has ever done before?"

"I do realize it, I also realize from what you've said that maybe the whole world is relying on us, and that's a lot of responsibility. Think about that before you celebrate."

Suddenly his visage turned decidedly stern before Mark answered her. "I have been thinking about it. Why do you think I left the command deck?"

She nodded, quietly now, and looked at him seriously, "Mark, I'm worried. This is big and I'm more than a little afraid. I know I'm not the only one."

Johnson smiled and reached to her, pulling her towards him, finally hugging her tightly. "Okay baby, I'll talk to the crew. Relax, we're going to be okay, I promise."

"All right." She returned his hug warmly, obviously frightened by what they just went through.

"Let's go back to the command deck ; I'll talk to everyone now."

"Okay." She replied.

Back on the command deck a minute later, Mark had Ariel cue up the comm system. "Crewmen of the Cagliostro, this is Mark Johnson, your Captain or boss or whatever you want to call me," he began, "I want to talk to you all about what we just went through. We were in a battle with a much larger star ship. We won, as I'm sure every one of you knows. Whether we just got lucky, or we won on smarts, I don't know, but the bottom line is we won. It's not something to be easily overlooked, or ignored. But we cannot let that go to our heads. To be honest I do not know what we are facing out here in the slightest. What lies in store for us is a mystery for me as well as for you. What I do know is that there will definitely be more trouble ahead of us. But there is no turning back. I know, we are not a military ship, but at the moment we are all that stands between our planet, Earth, and I don't know what. I do know there is something going on, and whatever it is, it's big. Big enough to be a danger to all of us and our families. No matter what, we have to see this through. Back home, everyone is counting on us, even if they do not know it. We have a mission to complete, let's do it as safely and smartly as possible. Johnson out." He motioned, and Ariel clicked off the comm unit, then Mark Johnson slumped back in his chair for a moment, steepling his fingers in front of his eyes while deep in thought. Out of everyone aboard Mark knew the most about what they were getting into, and as he had just begun to realize, in truth, he knew very little indeed.

The battle they had just fought did do one thing, and that was to raise his level of trepidation for what lie ahead.

Chapter Four

The Cagliostro sat in stationary orbit behind a moon on the frozen outskirts of an unknown solar system. The command crew sat within the command room, as Johnson began to brief them. "The fourth planet from this sun is an Earth-like world. It is in fact slightly hotter than Earth, and appears to be somewhat arid. It also seems to be a hub of activity. We have scanned dozens of ships coming and going from that planet. It is some sort of hot spot for activity. We have been monitoring all sub space communications in and out of that planet, and what we've been able to ascertain is that this planet is a commerce site for this galaxy. It's sort of a galactic hub. There is a large area that appears to be a military base located half the world away from the commerce area. As far as cities go, the commerce site is smaller than, say, New York, but it has a large space port nearby, on the outskirts of the area. We'll be taking the 'Stargrazer' there. The Cag will remain here behind this world hidden from that planet."

"How will we gain access to this place?" Red asked, pensively.

"Ariel's been scanning frequencies and through our translator we've been able to ascertain what we need to be allowed access. That part of it won't be a problem."

"Well that brings up another thing, how are we going to communicate with these people?" Eddie asked.

"I can answer that," Ariel interrupts, "Our suits have a translator circuit built in. we'll speak English, they'll answer in their language and we'll hear it in English. They will hear their language. Whatever the heck it is."

"How'd you come up with something like this, Mark? Heck how'd you even know where to begin?"

"Mark grinned boyishly, "Eddie, do you remember the old SETI program that had been searching for alien life for about five or six decades? The 'Search for Extraterrestrial Intelligence' had been sending queries into deep space over that time, and had been getting some replies, but didn't realize it until much later. I fed their data for the past half century through a mainframe I had developed that's sole purpose was language skills. It 'learned' everything SETI had 'heard' for years and was able to decipher certain things based upon what could be considered verbal punctuation. That same technology and what was deciphered previously is in our suits nano-computers, which are of course made of nano-bytes."

"What kind of place are we going to? You say it's a commerce spot, but what else do we know about it?" Red changed the subject.

"We really don't know anything about what we're walking into. Everyone packs a weapon, but keep them under your jackets, for now. If they try to take them from us, we reconvene at the Stargrazer and wait for everyone else's return. Then we all get the hell out of there. I'm, not allowing us to walk into an unknown city on an unknown planet without being armed. If we have to, we'll figure this out another way. I have to warn you all though, I'm putting us out there as targets as much as we are there looking for info. I want whoever is gunning for us to know we are there."

"So we have big bulls-eyes on our backs." Red observed.

"Pretty much, Red. We have to make sense of all of this. This may be the only way to do that."

Robinski nodded in agreement and sat back quietly.

"Anyone else have any questions or concerns?"

No one replied, as they looked at each other about the table.

"I'm not going to candy coat this for any of you. This is going to be dangerous."

They all nodded in understanding.

"All right. Gear up. Meet at the shuttle dock. The Stargrazer is being prepped right now, as we speak. We launch in fifty five minutes. See you all at the 'Grazer."

They all stood and exited the room talking amongst themselves. Ariel sidled up to Mark as the room emptied. "You know we're walking into a target range, right? This can't get any more dangerous."

"I already said that didn't I?" he answered with some annoyance.

"Relax tiger; I'm on your side."

"I know Ari. I wish I didn't need you at my side, but I do. Your telepathy will be a plus down there."

"Don't worry about me; I can take care of myself," she replied as she pulled her gun from its holster and checked its charge pack.

"Of that I have no doubt. There's goin to be a lot we'll have to watch down there. Do your best to screen out random thoughts and of course only look for thoughts centering on us."

"You do know we don't even know what the indigenous species looks like, right?"

Mark sighed, "Of course I do, Ari. C'mon let's get ready, maybe I'll even help you get dressed, if you're a bad girl that is."

"Oooo, I can be bad, I can be very bad." She fluffed her long, wavy blonde hair and cooed in his ear as they exited the conference room. All the while Mark Johnson fought a feeling of overwhelming dread as they entered Ariel's quarters.

***

Less than an hour later the entire command crew was gathered in the shuttle bay as Johnson and Ariel joined them. There were several small shuttle ships within the docking bay, and one larger, sleeker craft. It had a rounded nose and wings that jutted out from its sides and swept back on rounded curves resolving in points at the back of the ship. The craft was a gleaming beauty; beneath it two of the magno-disc engines spun slowly as pre-flight testing was being completed. The ship was large enough to hold six crew and supplies for any extended spaceflight, including bunks and sleeping quarters.

"Are we ready to go?" Mark asked as he walked up the entry ramp into the smaller ship.

"Just about." Dan Sledge replied from within the Stargrazer. "Performing final pre-flight checklist right now."

"Very good Dan. Let's get aboard and settled in."

The others followed, carrying duffle bags over their shoulders, filled with a few days' clothes and gear.

Within minutes they were strapped into their chairs on the command deck of the small ship which was really only one level, with the storage space and sleeping quarters behind the command deck or flight bridge.

Mark and Dan sat in the two forward chairs and worked virtual control interfaces powering up the ships engines. Instantly the ship rose up off the deck and slowly moved towards what appeared to be a garage door, which began to rise as they approached it.

Mark thumbed the communicator control and instantly was in contact with the Cagliostro's command deck. "Mr. Jefferson, we are about to leave the Cagliostro, are you firmly in command of my ship?"

The view screen on the console before Mark sprang to life, and Miles Jefferson, a young black man smiled as his visage filled the screen. Behind him, the secondary command crew began running through the Cagliostro's diagnostics as every command crew did upon starting their shift. "We're all set on our end Captain, we'll take care of your ship, I promise. Good hunting, boss!"

Mark smiled aboard the Stargrazer and he replied, "Thanks Miles, hopefully we'll be the hunters and not the huntees."

With that the Stargrazer exited the Cagliostro's shuttle deck and disappeared into the depths of space, accelerating towards the fourth planet from the systems sun.

"Anything we oughta know about this place?" Dan Sledge asked.

"It's hot down there." Red replied, "Like a hundred and five in the shade, but it's like Arizona, a dry heat." He snickered sarcastically.

"Our uniforms will keep us cool enough," Mark began, stealing an annoyed glance at Red, "the thermal venting system will pull the heat from our bodies keeping us at least ten degrees cooler than our surroundings. It's not much but it's better than nothing. The ships hatch will be code locked to each of our suits. Only we can enter and exit. They'll have to cut through the hatch to get into her. So we should be safe from thieves and spies, I hope." He added.

The Stargrazer sped towards the planet in question, exiting hyper-warp just past the planet's first moons trajectory. Casually Ariel thumbed up the comm and began speaking, "This is the 'Stargrazer' requesting permission to land at the spaceport in region 2.5 on planetary grid."

There was no answer at first. She tilted her head quizzically and shrugged her shoulders towards Mark, who waved his hand as if to say 'relax'. The comm unit suddenly sprang to life as alien words were barked from it several times before the translator was able to catch up, matching inflection with syntax, until the beings voice on the other side suddenly became clear.

"This is space port command for spaceport Z-59; please state your business here," the voice ordered.

Ariel immediately replied, "This is the Spaceship Stargrazer requesting permission to land. We are seeking additional provisions for our extended journey back to our own solar system, as well as a few days rest on a planet's surface among other races and peoples."

The voice was silent a moment, then two, as if having a conversation with someone nearby before finally replying, "Very well Stargrazer, proceed to landing pad N-157. A landing beam will guide you in."

"Thank you, Spaceport command." Ariel answered before thumbing off the communications unit.

"We're in." She offered to Mark.

"Yeah, I know." He paused a second then added, "That's what I'm worried about."

"Why are you worried?" Ariel asked.

"It seems a bit too easy. They have no idea who we are or where we're from, yet they have no trouble at all inviting us in. I expected a bit more resistance to our landing here, that's all."

The landing beam made contact with the little ship before it broke atmosphere and helped direct them as they began its descent. The Stargrazer descended through the atmosphere, as the heat of reentry made the wings glow on either side of the sleek craft, turning them a bright yellow with heat, before they finally cooled as the ship slowed enough and vectored into its heading towards the spaceport.

Soon, the 'grazer was slowing enough that it shed all of the excess heat it had built up upon re-entry. Some had been converted to energy and stored, but the powerful magno-disc engines created energy for power as well as flight ability. It was a win-win science. Within minutes the ship hovered above a landing spot and descended for a feather soft vertical landing.

"Should we take our bags with us?" Eddie asked.

"No, the plan is to stay here tonight, within the ship. I'm not interested in looking for whatever passes as an inn at least for a day or two. Let's do some shopping and see what supplies we can actually come up with in this place. Everyone take your universal scanners with you and scan everything you consider buying or whatever the heck we're going to call it here. We have to know what is in everything we're touching here. Again our suits will protect us, to a point."

They all nodded silently as they clipped their holsters to their uniforms and slid their energy pistols into them. The universal scanners went on their left hip.

"Everyone ready?" Mark asked.

They all replied affirmatively. Mark touched the ramp and door control. Instantly the door slid up and the ramp slid down to the ground. They walked out smiling and chatting amiably amongst themselves, putting on a perfect display of a crew that needed some time away from being cooped up in a small ship for a long time.

Around them, human-like aliens worked about the other spacecrafts parked in stalls surrounding the Stargrazer. Their skin color was dark, but purple, not what Earthmen would associate with a dark colored skin. Their hair, if you could call it that, looked more like varying shades of lettuce then hair. The workers momentarily eyed the Stargrazer's crew suspiciously, and then returned to their business.

Mark punched a code into the ships door lock pad and the hatchway sealed up behind them, leaving the ramp to the ground in place.

"Man, you were right about this place being hot." Eddie wiped his brow before replacing his blue baseball cap once they were out of the Stargrazer's shade.

"Yeah ain't that the truth." Sledge dropped a pair of sunglasses in place, and popped a baseball cap atop his own head. The blue and white caps read "USS Stargrazer".

"Let's head into that market we saw from above as we were landing. Remember, let's not look for trouble, I have a feeling it's going to find us easy enough."

"If it does I'll be ready." Red fingered his gun within its holster.

"Take it easy there, Wyatt Earp," Dan chided, "We may not run into any trouble an' if we do, I got yer back. So don't sweat it and let's not look for it."

Red nodded stoically to Dan as they continued to walk. The streets were packed sand and the bright sandy color permeated everything as far as the eye could see.

"This ain't exactly a garden spot, huh boss?" Eddie asked.

"Not in the least Eddie, not in the least."

Ariel kept quiet but was doing far more than ignoring her comrade's banter. She gently probed those around them as they walked, listening in with her psychic ability for anything that would be of use to them.

The group walked up to what could loosely be termed as a supermarket, which they entered through the deflector field doors. The doors served two purposes, one the deflector fields kept insects and other vermin out, and it also kept the air conditioned air in.

"What is this place?" Eddie asked as he looked around.

"What? The town?" Dan answered.

"Yeah, weird place. Lots of different species walking around, most are humanoid, but some definitely aren't."

"Not what I'm talking about Dan. This town, what is it? I mean it's a rundown spaceport town, I get that, but something else is going on here. People live here. I'm seeing all run down one story buildings and homes. But there are a lot of ships in that spaceport. Nothing big, mostly ships about the size of the 'Grazer. But something draws them here. What is it?"

"Good question Eddie," Mark replied quietly, "Ariel, anything?"

"No. Not a thing. People are curious about us, but that's about it. I'm not reading any hostile thoughts so far, just curiosity. Oh and by the way, this food here seems to be mostly edible for us, so far. Lots of different fruits here that resemble earthly melons and oranges and the like. Some meats here appear to be this world's equivalent of cattle. Again, edible. Some other stuff I just came across I wouldn't touch."

"Okay Ari, Thanks." Mark answered, "Let's maybe not be so inconspicuous now."

"Whaddaya got in mind boss?" Red asked.

"What's the best place to go for information on a new town, to get the lay of the land and what not?"

"Where else?" Red replied, "A bar."

"Bingo." Mark winked as he exited the market.

Ariel paid for the few items they picked up with gold coins Mark had them each carry. Gold it seemed was still the universal coin, literally.

A few seconds later Ariel and Red, who had stayed with her within the shop, re-joined the rest of the crew outside.

"So where're we gonna find a bar in this dump?" Dan asked as he moved his big frame through the crowded streets.

"That's easy Danny-boy," Mark replied with a sly grin, "Just follow the music."

The five adventurers did just that, wending their way through busy, sand covered streets clogged with dusty people. They exited into a wide thoroughfare where what could only peripherally be called music could be heard from a number of establishments. One gathering spot was larger than the rest, and seemed the busiest, with the most raucous crowd.

"What do you think?" Red asked Mark.

"I think this is the place we want."

The group of five entered the establishment and looked around. It was a dimly lit, smoke filled place, packed with different aliens. Plenty wore different uniforms, some just dusty work type clothes. A band played something that was barely melodic to say the least, and which seemed mostly ignored by the clientele who sat in small clusters and talked amongst themselves at dark tables. A few of the purple skinned indigenous females were out on the dance floor with a few men of differing species.

Johnson led his people to a round table in a corner of the bar. They all sat down.

"Now what?" Eddie looked around the room from under the brim of his hat.

"Now we wait." Mark Johnson answered.

They did not have to wait long. A waitress finally sauntered up to the table they were sitting at, an electronic pad in her hands. She spoke in a tongue no one understood, but after a second the translators within their suits compensated and the words she spoke were finally heard in English.

"Whadaya wanna drink?" She asked in a surly tone.

"You have ale?" Mark asked.

She laughed sarcastically, "Yeah I got twenty seven different kinds."

"Give us the most popular one. Five mugs." Mark ordered.

She nodded, smiled, and walked off.

"Not sure if she was friendly or not." Dan commented.

"She was indifferent, as in just doing her job." Ariel replied.

"I guess that's better than the alternative." Red commented.

"So what now?" Red asked in a conspirational whisper.

"Now we wait and take in the show. Have patience. Someone will be interested in us soon enough." Mark Johnson replied.

"I hate it when you're right." Ariel replied, as she turned her head towards the bar itself where two men sat trying not to act like they were staring at the newcomers.

"What have you got?" Mark asked.

"Those two have been watching us the last few minutes. They followed us in from the street. They must have been tailing us for a while, but with all the white noise out there I only heard them clearly when they came in here."

"That's funny, I'd a thought it would have been worse in here." Eddie smirked.

"No it's more condensed in here. Actually there are less people in here than on that street and the ones here are all interested in finding a mate for the evening."

"In other words, hooking up." Eddie finished.

"You got it ace." Ariel smiled and nodded.

"So what are they thinking about us?" Red asked.

"They know what we are, where we're from. I distinctly heard the word 'Earth' in my mind. Right now they're just curious it seems, but I do sense malevolence on their parts."

"Okay, let's see how long it takes them to come over and say hello."

The two men were humanoids, but not from the planet they were all currently on. Both were big beings, with flat faces and bald heads, soft ridges started at their brows and went over the tops of their heads to their necks. Their skin color was a dull red. They each wore a dull brown coverall.

The waitress returned with the mugs of ale. Mark paid her in a few gold coins. A moment later she returned with change in a coin of a smaller size, then disappeared into the crowd.

"I have no idea what we just paid for these drinks but I have a feeling it was too much." He commented with a slight laugh as he took a sip and shook his head up and down on an angle. "Not bad actually. I think this'll do for now, gents."

"How long do we wait for our admirers to join us?" Red asked as he drank his ale.

"As long as it takes, we're explorers enjoying some down time out of our ship. Remember, we're Earthmen who knew of alien life before but never met anyone of other worlds ourselves."

Sledge looked at Mark "That is the truth you know, boss."

"I know Danny. Let's just keep all our cards hidden for now and play this hand warily."

Red shook his head and scowled, "I hate poker analogies."

"That's 'cause your poker game sucks." Eddie chided Red, with a quick smirk.

"Quiet," Ariel hissed, "they're coming over now to find out about us."

"Ari if you hear anything underhanded in their minds while they're talking to us, tell us through your telepathy."

'*Will do, Mark.*' Her mental voice rang through their minds in a bell-like tone.

The two burly aliens walked to the end of the teams table and stood there, with what looked like an attempt at a smile on each of their faces. Finally, the one on the right started to speak.

"Greetings, I am Endorf and this is Credom. We noticed you sitting here but were unaware of your species. We have never seen anyone that looked exactly like you do. Where do you hail from?"

'*That's a lie, they know exactly where we're from.*' The bell-like mental voice of Ariel pinged through their minds.

"We're explorers from a small planet several light years from here. What about you two gentlemen? Where are you from?"

"We are from a world known as Tanzi-7. It is some light years from here. What brings you beings to this place?"

Mark held up his mug and smiled, "The ale. We heard it was good here and decided to check it out for ourselves."

The alien on the left stared on with a perplexed look upon his face.

"Seriously?" He asked.

His companion nudged him with an elbow, and then resumed smiling at the team, "I beg your indulgence, you must ignore my friend here, he does not get out much."

"That's quite all right, Endorf." Mark replied congenially, "Why don't you and your friend sit down and join us for a drink."

Both aliens nodded, after looking to the other and sat at the end of the table, each ordering a flagon of the ale everyone else was drinking.

"So I'm curious, what do you two gents do here? You both have what appear to be work coveralls on, at least to my untrained eye. Are you ship mechanics?" Mark asked.

"Yes that we are. We actually saw you land here earlier today."

"Ah okay, so how'd you like our ship? It's the first of its kind."

"It's very nice." Credom replied enthusiastically enough that Endorf gave him another nudge in the ribs immediately.

"We like it just fine," the seemingly more intelligent of the two replied.

Mark leaned forward, almost surreptitiously, and then asked,. "Have either of you ever seen anyone like us before? We're looking for a lost friend. He's going to look very much like us, with our skin tone and hair type."

"No, I cannot say that we have, I must apologize. You are the first of your kind we have ever seen."

'*Another lie.*' Ariel's voice rang in their skulls.

Mark shrugged and smiled, "Ah well, it was worth a try. So let me ask you two, what passes for entertainment on this world? Is there anything worth seeing here, while we relax for a few days?"

"Well the matches here are really fun." Credom answered dully.

"What matches?" Dan replied.

"Those matches." Endorf replied.

'*It's some kind of gladiatorial events within this bar.*' Ariel's voice sang lightly across their minds.

As she replied, two bruisers made their way into the ring that was on the left of the bar itself, which had been hidden the whole time by the mass of bodies within the place. Now it was clearly visible as people cleared out of the way to let the two fighters through. Both were surly looking louts. Big and angry with plenty of scars and tattoos across their bodies which could be seen plainly as they entered the ring, pulling the ropes down as they stepped over them on opposite sides of the ring.

"These guys are big." Red offered.

"That means they really are big, if you're saying so." Eddie smirked.

Red shot him an annoyed look that clearly said 'shut up'.

Sitting back in his chair Mark kept one eye on his guests, and another on the ring behind them. The combatants were clearly two different races. One was a scaled lizard man from God only knew where. The other looked almost like a bear, with a thick coat of fur covering his body from head to toe. His arms were longer than the lizard mans by almost a foot, but the lizard seemed somewhat bulkier looking.

"This should be interesting." Red sneered.

"Yeah, I'm kinda looking forward to this myself." Dan agreed.

'*Don't lose track of what we are here for.*' Ariel's thoughts chimed in everyone's mind.

'*No chance of that Ari.*' Mark replied mentally, knowing by her smile that she heard him.

Within the ring the two big combatants circled each other, each looking for an opening.

Suddenly the lizard-man lunged at his hairy opponent, who met the charge head on with a savage grunt. They grappled momentarily, until the bear-like creature ducked below the reptilian one's slashing arms and caught his foe in a crushing embrace, then stood up quickly and heaved his enemy into the air. As the reptile came down haphazardly the bear-like creature lashed out with two quick blows, left-right in the blink of an eye, even before the reptilian landed upon his back on the canvas of the ring.

Now everyone at their table, including the two strangers were totally engrossed in the battle.

The hairy behemoth charged the reptile again, just as he was getting to his clawed feet, when the reptile grabbed his enemy by the throat and spit some vile venom into his foes eyes. The bear-man stumbled backwards, frantically clawing at his eyes in pain, as he lizard attacked again, biting the bear-like creature on the shoulder, spraying its blood across the ring as the hairy brute howled in pain and dropped to the mat, unconscious.

"My God!" Shouted Eddie, "I don't think I've ever seen anything that incredible before."

"At least not that brutal." Ariel replied, disgusted.

"That was…interesting to say the least." Dan added.

Mark shook his head with a slight smile, "Mmm-hhmm."

"There are no rules here," Endorf began, joining the conversation, "Short of killing, which is not allowed. It is a brutal sport, but the people like it." He shrugged as he finished his comment.

"Yes we like it, we even fight sometimes ourselves." Credom added.

"You don't look any worse for the wear of it." Red noticed.

Endorf smiled and leaned forward at this, displaying a tightly packed row of small, sharp teeth, "That is because we win."

'*Watch it; I'm getting all kinds of thoughts from both of them, images of them brutally beating opponents.*' Ariel's mental voice sang.

"Well, why doesn't one of you fight the winner here, and give us newcomers a show?" Mark asked with a genial smile.

"What do we get when we win?" Credom asked.

"I'll wager a few gold pieces on you." Mark replied, leaning in.

"Not enough, we want your ship." Endorf sneered. "We win, we get your ship."

"That's crazy." Eddie replied, leaning back in his chair.

"Not gonna happen." Dan answered, grim faced, Red nodded in agreement, as both stared menacingly at the two aliens seated with them.

"What's in it for us?" Mark prodded, with his eyes slit, and his lips set grimly.

"We have much information you might want." Endorf smiled again in answer.

'Watch it, he's baiting you Mark. I can't get a clear read on his alien mind but there is something there. Something he feels we'd want to know.' Ariel mentally informed the crew.

"It had better be *very* important information if you think I'm willing to lose the only means we have of getting off this sandbar," Mark answered in a hiss.

"It's very big; you would want to know what we know."

"You're asking a lot to expect me to trust your word about some nameless information and wager it against my ship."

"What I have you want, I promise." Endorf replied, almost greasily.

'Mark, you can't seriously be thinking of taking this guy at his word can you?' Ariel hissed mentally.

'Relax,' He replied through her mind-link, *'Worse comes to worse the Cag comes and gets us all after a few days, I have no intention of letting the Stargrazer fall into anyone's hands. Let alone these two morons.'*

He turned back towards Endorf, "You have to give me something up front so I know your information is worthwhile. If it's not worth my time, I'm not going to be bothered."

Endorf smiled then and leaned towards Mark to whisper something to him. Mark's face shifted almost imperceptibly at the red brute's words, then he sat back in his chair, his brow furrowed in thought. Next to Mark, Ariel did her best to hide what she had mentally heard, as she shifted her head towards the arena once again, her blonde hair trailing after her turned face in one quick motion. Her face, now hidden from the rest of the table showed immediate concern.

Mark faced Endorf, and his face was unreadable, merely set, as he began to speak. "All right your terms are fine, but hear me and understand what I'm saying here; if you try to cheat us, well, it will not be a good move on your part. That's something to think about before we enter into this little wager, and be assured we *will* know if there's any deception on your part."

The big alien nodded slowly and grinned, relaxing back in his chair, as the ring announcer continued to call out for challengers to the reptilian who had just beaten the bear-like creature.

Endorf raised his hand and whistled so that he drew the announcers' attention, "Credom will battle the Zrigg. He will challenge him."

'*Mark, this is bad, terribly bad.*' Ariel warned through the mind link, '*The crowd is already getting worked up at Credom's name alone.*'

Credom stood up and grinned at the group seated with him, it was not a pleasant site. It bespoke more of "I got you" then anything pleasant.

Ariel again broke into their thoughts, '*Mark...*'

'*Ssshhh.*' He replied in a mental hiss the team all heard.

The red skinned brute walked up to the ring and pulled the ropes down, stepping over them. The Zrigg, if that was his name or race, no one among them but the two strangers knew, merely snorted contemptuously at his new enemy.

Both alien creatures circled each other menacingly, and then Credom charged, right into the right fist of the Zrigg, who knocked him over like a bowling pin. Credom shook his head and fought to his knees as the Zrigg suddenly streaked up to him and kicked him in the gut, sending him sprawling again.

'*He's desperate.*' Red said, through the mind link.

'*Who? Credom?*' Eddie replied mentally.

'*No, the Zrigg. He's trying to end this as fast as possible.*

They said nothing verbally, but sat stone still watching as Endorf merely grinned.

Credom was on one knee now as the Zrigg continued to pound at him, raining blows continuously on the red skinned powerhouse, and changing his position every few seconds, just staying out of reach as his downed foe tried and failed repeatedly to get to his feet.

The Zrigg reached in to punch Credom in the head once again, when suddenly the kneeling red skinned alien caught the hand before it could descend upon him once more, and he grinned. A heartbeat later he twisted the hand ruthlessly, and stood up, shoving the bewildered Zrigg away from himself, as if he were but a child.

Then, with a maddened howl, Credom charged forward and attacked the Zrigg, who ran to meet the charge head on, literally. The two smashed heads together with a loud bang.

The lizard man stumbled feeling his forehead, as he woozily backed away. Credom merely laughed as he leapt atop the wounded Zrigg and hammered him with powerful, unrelenting blows that literally shook the arena with their thunder.

The Zrigg tried to spit his venom into Credom's face, but the red skinned brute merely lowered his head so that the venom splashed across his ridged skull.

Credom had the Zrigg pinned on the mat floor when he raised both hands together above his head in twin fists. He brought them down atop the defenseless Zrigg with such explosive fury that the ring they were standing in collapsed from the power of the blow. Dust and sand filled the bar, obscuring the vision of everyone. The ventilation system quickly kicked into high gear, fighting to clear the air.

Finally, from within the cloud of dust a shadowed figure could be seen holding another in one hand above its head triumphantly. As the fans sucked the dust and sand from the air, Credom contemptuously tossed the prone form of the Zrigg to what was left of the arena mat, like so much garbage.

Endorf turned towards Mark with his hand extended and a smile from ear hole to ear hole,

"Your ship, please?"

Chapter Five

Ariel, Eddie, Red and Dan sat there tensely, as if they were controlled by a hair trigger. Each was ready to spring to the attack in their own manner. Mark merely smiled at the big red skinned alien before him who continued to hold his hand out before him.

"What? You expect me to just hand you the keys to the ship without us having a chance to win it back first?"

"You made a deal." Endorf grunted angrily through gritted teeth.

"Yes and we'll abide by it, but you are going to at least give us a chance to go double or nothing, right?"

"What else have you got to wager?"

"What else do you want?" Mark replied with a slight grin.

Endorf thought a second, then with a twisted grin replied, "The Female. She will bring good credits in the slave market."

Ariel leaped up from her chair, almost at the same time as Red and Dan, "Are you kidding me? I'm not even going to listen to this garbage," she barked.

"Relax, Ariel. Sit down." Mark ordered, grinning like a Cheshire cat.

'*You're okay with this?*' She asked him incredulously with her telepathic voice.

'*Trust me, I've never let you down, I won't now. This creep is not getting his greasy paws on you, I promise you. Trust me.*' He replied through the same mind link.

'*Why do I always dread those words?*'

"So you want Ariel, eh?"

Endorf nodded slowly, "As humans go, she is comely. Not to my eyes, of course but as far your species, she is…adequate." He grinned now.

"I don't like this, but very well. So how do we go about this then?" Mark asked. Eyeing the red skinned mountain of muscle before him warily.

"How else? You fight! Credom awaits!" Endorf spread his right arm and aimed it wide at Credom who stood by the ring as it was being repaired, and the unconscious Zrigg carried off.

"You want me, to fight him?" Mark asked, wide eyed.

"What other way is there, little human?" Endorf laughed hysterically, his voice sounding like granite plates grinding together loudly. Spittle dripped from his jaws uncontrollably as his big red shoulders bounced up and down with joy.

"Okay, fine you want a fight, you got one. But I'm not going to do the fighting here." The big alien began to protest as Mark raised a hand stopping him. "You want Ariel as your winning piece; I'm totally against that, where we come from slavery is not tolerated in any way shape or form. One sentient creature owning another is barbaric and absolutely deplorable."

"And yet it is your only bargaining chip that I will accept."

Ariel looked at Mark cautiously, in his mind he said *'Relax, I've got this.'*

"I hope you know what you're doing." She answered for all to hear, verbally.

"So who do you propose to fight in your stead, human?"

Red began to stand, cracking his knuckles as a wicked smile cracked across his lips.

Mark grabbed his arm and sat him back down. "Not you Red, and no buts." Mark turned to Dan Sledge and nodded with a wicked grin of his own.

Dan stood and nodded once to his friends, then turned and walked towards the fighting ring.

'I gotta tell you Mark, I'm against this.' Red growled over the mental link, *'This is my job, not Dan's.'*

'I need you here, Red. There's a reason.'

'You mean besides the fact that he's a hundred times stronger than me, or anyone else that we know of?'

'Well, there is that, mostly.' Mark admitted.

'Even so I'm the better fighter, you know that.'

'Yes you are, but with his strength he doesn't have to be. Now let's watch the show, this should be interesting, and keep an eye on our pal here, in case he tries to bolt out of here.' Mark answered mentally.

Dan Sledge entered the newly repaired ring, stepping over the ropes and facing his foe.

Credom sneered at him, "Little human, I will try not to hurt you, much. I know how delicate your species is."

Then, like lightning, the alien struck at Sledge, its bright red fist slashing forward and smacking Dan across the jaw.

But Dan Sledge's reaction was not what Credom expected, not by half. Dan stood his ground and smirked, rubbing his jaw with the back of his hand. Credom quickly threw a right cross at Dan, who blocked it with his left arm, and then retaliated with a lightning fast attack of his own. His right fist shot out, as if from a cannon, and struck Credom's jaw with such force that the red skinned brute shot across the ring and collided with the cables on the opposite side, and then fell to the mat like a puppet with its strings cut.

Credom was stunned. He was lying on the mat and slowly got to all fours unsteadily as Dan stood back, giving him room. The alien stood shakily, and shook his head one time then charged Dan, ramming into his mid-section head first with his bony skull.

But where this would normally have guaranteed Credom a victory against anyone else, against Dan Sledge it was like running into a mountain. Credom rolled over, out cold before he hit the mat.

A deafening cheer went up all through the bar as the patrons celebrated in disbelief.

Slowly, surreptitiously, Endorf made his way to his feet and looked side to side, before turning and quickly, especially for someone so large, headed toward the exit.

Sledge exited the arena and walked back towards the table. What he saw made him run the last few feet towards his friends.

"You're not going anywhere!" Red shouted as he held Endorf by the collar, and forced back against the wall. Eddie stood across from Endorf with his pistol trained on him while the bartender shouted "No Blasters!"

"Uhh, Best out of three?" Endorf replied with a sheepish grin.

"I think not." Mark replied. Now it was his turn to smile like the fox in a hen house. "I want that information you promised. No more games."

"A-all right." The defeated alien replied while looking at the humans before him, their weapons held at the ready.

"You Earth men are tougher then you look."

"Who ever said we were from Earth? We didn't." Red growled.

Endorf gulped hard at this and looked around for some avenue of escape, but he'd run out of options.

"Sit back down and let's talk." Mark nodded at the table and the burly alien took his seat again. He looked visibly uncomfortable as his companion was carried away from the arena in front of their table on a stretcher. Dan took a seat on one side of Endorf and Red on the other. Both smiled at the alien, but their smiles were without mirth.

"Now as we were saying. What do you know about Earth?"

"Uh, I know that a ship came here a while back. A few months, by how we count time on this world. There was a man who looked like you people, an Earthman. He was taken out of the spaceport quietly, and under guard. No one asked questions. There were a lot of credits passed around to make sure of that. Very few saw him come and go. Credom and I did because we were working maintenance on a ship that had to be repaired by the following morning."

"So you saw the whole thing? Why weren't you made to shut up about it? How'd you escape notice?" Red asked, face to face with the big alien.

Endorf snorted, "Heh. You're not as stupid as you look, are you? They never saw us. We were back in the repair bay of the spaceport and they brought him through there to avoid crowds. It was long past work hours were over. We shouldn't have been there at all. But Credom saw them coming and it just looked wrong. No one ever comes through the repair center, especially at night, at least not that late. So we both hid inside the ship we were working on, and watched silently. We saw them hustling this guy through here. I think he was old as you people go. His fur was white, an' he had a patch of fur over his mouth."

"Wait a minute," Eddie interjected, "Was this guy kinda heavy? Like round around the middle?"

"He was."

"Did you hear a name? Did they talk to him at all? Did they call him anything?" Mark pressed.

"They called him, like I told you before, the General."

"Did you see where they went when they left the spaceport? What'd they leave in?"

"You losers really aren't too bright are ya?" The alien laughed gruffly. "He was their prisoner. They were laughin' at him. His hands were tied in front of him. They pushed him into a hover car an' took off."

"And you have no idea where they went, do you?" Red grunted.

"Up north. To the mountainous regions a few hundred clicks that way." He waved his hand in a direction behind his head.

"Let's all take a walk back to the spaceport." Mark commanded and everyone stood at once. "Endorf, pay the bill."

Endorf sneered as he laid the credits on the table for the waitress. "Make sure you tip her good." Red growled. The alien started to protest as Dan placed his hand on the red skinned brutes shoulder and squeezed, just enough to make his point.

The entire group walked back out into the street and headed towards the spaceport a few blocks away.

"What are you?" Endorf asked Dan as they walked.

"It's complicated. Leave it at that." Dan replied gruffly.

"I ain't never seen anything like you. No one 'round here can match Credom an' me in strength. Yet you're stronger than we are. How's that even possible?"

"You better learn pal, that no matter how bad you are, there's always someone badder." Dan replied.

"So where we goin' now?" Endorf continued talking.

"Now you are coming with us aboard our ship and we're going to fly up into those mountains and find that man you saw."

Endorf stopped in his tracks. "No. I can't do that. I'm not authorized to travel out of this area, and you can't take a ship out of here and fly that way. All space fairing vessels have to stay here within the spaceport. Them's the rules. Plus I ain't allowed anywhere outta the commercial zone."

"Why not? Were you a bad boy?" Eddie grinned sarcastically.

"I'm a worker here, on a work visa. I live nearby. Credom an' I stay here for six months at a time then go home to our planet. Then we come back for another six months. The credits are good." He shrugged.

"So are all the goodies you and your pal lie, cheat and steal people out of, I'd wager." Mark replied sardonically.

Again the big alien shrugged, but this time with a smirk.

"Uh guys…" Ariel stopped them with a hand raised. *'I'm getting thoughts aimed at us and our ship from within the hangar.'* She told them mentally.

Eddie, being the smallest member of the crew—besides Ariel—slunk around the nearest corner and peered over at their ship through the shadows. "Sunova…" He began.

"What is it?" Mark pushed.

"The Stargrazer, it's surrounded, by guys in uniforms. The purple skinned, salad heads." He turned back and looked at Mark, "The ship's cordoned off."

"What's going on here Endorf? I want answers now." Mark hissed.

"Uhh, security has surrounded your ship?"

"That much I can tell. Why, though? What set them off?"

'They knew we were coming.' Ariel's voice sang across their minds once again.

'How?' Mark replied mentally.

'The plant or traitor or whatever he is. That's the only explanation.' Red offered.

'So they've been waiting for us. Then those ships that attacked us on the way here were not pirates or thieves or some other random act.'

'Are you Earthmen that naïve that you believe those were random attacks?' a new mental voice forced its way

into their mind link. Immediately, Ariel fell to her knees holding her head with both hands and moaned piteously. Mark ran to her and grabbed her by the shoulders.

Behind the group a creature appeared that lay an aura of dread upon everyone there. Even Endorf began to babble and mutter as he backed away from the thing, wide eyed and fear filled.

The creature stood eight feet tall, but it was gaunt. Thin as a whisper at sunset. Its skin was a burnt brown color. Its scalp was three sharp boned rows running front to back. The thing then stretched a questing hand towards Endorf. Even as it did so the length of that impossibly long hand and fingers were the first thing one noticed. They were twice the length of a tall man's hand and had four joints instead of two. It wore a black uniform with white frilled cuffs and collar. Endorf backed away fearfully. Immediately Red positioned himself between the nightmarish horror and Endorf, even as Ariel continued to squirm upon the ground.

"Let her go, now!" Mark roared as he threw himself at the creature before them. Obviously the thing, whatever it was, was not prepared for Johnson's head long rush as he bowled it over easily, tackling it and sending it smashing to the ground. He drew his fist back and began pummeling it relentlessly.

Ariel was instantly back on her feet, backing away from the creature with fearful eyes. Dan immediately grasped her to him protectively. "What'd that thing do to you?" He asked quietly, fearfully.

"I-I have never felt anything like that. It just took control of my mind. My thoughts were all its own. I couldn't form a coherent thought of my own. I-it showed me terrible things. I was helpless."

"What is that thing?" Red asked as he stood there with his gun drawn on it.

"That is a Quel." A new voice intruded. They all turned towards its source, back towards the Stargrazer, where a purple skinned being was walking towards them with its hands behind its back. It wore a uniform of some kind. "They are nasty creatures, we employ them when we fear telepaths are involved. They, as your woman now knows, can worm their way into a telepaths mind and gain control of it. They are indeed horrid creatures, but infinitely useful. You may all drop your weapons now, we have you surrounded."

Mark stopped hitting the foul smelling creature beneath him and looked around. Eddie and Red continued to hold their guns at the ready, damned sure they weren't going to go down without a fight. Dan held Ariel steady, who was still shaky on her feet. They were indeed surrounded by uniformed men, whether military or security of some kind Mark could not distinguish.

While all eyes were upon the Stargrazer's crew, Endorf turned and ran. The man in charge made a quick motion with his hand, his fingers pointing at the fleeing red skinned alien brute, and then quickly slashing across his throat, as several energy blasts rang out, all connecting with the fleeing mechanics back, dropping him to the cement floor, his body smoldering.

Once more with his hands behind his back the purple skinned humanoid creature turned to face the crew.

"You will be coming with us, are there any more questions?"

Chapter Six

Mark stood slowly as all eyes were trained on him. The men surrounding them watched him nervously. The Quel lay upon the ground, unconscious and bloody. Mark made eye contact with Red, and then moved his eyes towards the Stargrazer.

"Well? Move along, all of you." The alien officer ordered.

"Why? What'd we do?" Eddie asked, stalling.

"You will ask no questions alien. You will simply come with us. Move along now. That is an order."

"I don't think so, now drop your weapons. I really don't want to kill any of you." Mark replied with a wicked smile.

"You seem to have some misconception based on your situation. We outnumber you and all our weapons are trained upon you."

"And my ships guns are trained on you. Drop your weapons and stand down now. Or the ship will take you all out."

"You lie, Earthling."

"Another guy who knows where we're from?" Eddie asked.

"Yeah, looks that way, Eddie." Mark answered while not taking his eyes off their antagonist. "Seems this guy knows who we are, and on that he has us at a disadvantage. But that's all. Drop your guns now officer, or whatever you are."

"Prepare to fire." The purple alien barked. "Your bluff has been called, Earthman."

"It's no bluff." Mark replied, smiling as the gun on the wing of the Stargrazer barked a blue bolt of light, smacking the alien officer in the back and dropping him to the pavement.

The men surrounding the crew all looked towards the ship and prepared to fire when Mark spoke up again.

"All of you lay down your weapons and surrender. Last chance."

Now all the troops looked around between the crew, who still had their guns drawn and aimed at them, and then back at the ship whose wing guns were also aimed at the troopers.

Suddenly an energy blast rang out at the teams back, shaking the ground, throwing them from their feet and making them cover their heads and faces as chunks of debris and concrete sprayed about them.

Mark was on his feet immediately, grabbing Ariel by the arm and running her directly towards the Stargrazer while shouting, "Run! Back to the ship, now!"

Behind them hovered an open air craft with two big guns mounted on it. Within it behind blast proof twin windscreens, two troopers were ready to fire again. Red and Eddie begin firing their hand guns at the ship, their laser bolts sprayed across the ship's hull with little damage.

Dan Sledge suddenly started to run towards the small hovering gunship, building speed as he went with each lumbering step, "You heard the Boss, get back to the ship, I got this."

"What the hell?" Red shouted as Dan leaped into the air, sailing forty feet into the sky above the small hovering gunship, then he dropped down onto and through the vessel, feet first with his knees pulled up to his chest. As he landed, he slammed them down into the craft, breaking through it like tissue paper, and turning it to rubble in one explosive maneuver.

Now the troopers begin to scatter and run as the Stargrazer powered up and lifted off its landing pad, turning towards their enemies in midair.

Dan Sledge walked towards Red and Eddie, wiping dust from his hands, grinning ear to ear.

Red looked at him, grimaced and shook his head side to side, "I hate you, you know that right?"

Dan laughed and slapped his friend on the back, "C'mon, both of you, let's get to the ship. There're gonna be more o' these clowns gettin' here any sec."

They ran towards the 'Grazer as Red reiterated, "I do you know, I really do," with a grin.

"Get on board, willya?" Sledge grunted, smiling.

Red, Dan and Eddie ran up the entry ramp as it started to withdraw into the ship behind them.

"What are we going to do Mark?" Ariel asked.

"Get out of here for now. That's a start."

The ship powered up and streaked skyward as behind them two more of the two seat gunships began to pursue them.

"They're firing on us Mark." Red remarked.

As if to underscore his statement the Stargrazer rumbled twice as energy blasts slapped against its skin.

"Do we fire back on them?" Eddie asked as he readied his weapons console.

"No, these we can outrun. Let's play it that way, for now."

Eddie nodded, "Alright Mark. It's your call."

"Dan get us out of here, fast."

Sledge nodded, "You got it, boss."

The Stargrazer shot away from the planet, rocketing into space, leaving the two pursuit ships instantly far behind.

The Stargrazer blasted away from the planet, and toward a moon, one of four in orbit of the planet.

"Stationary orbit behind the moon, then we contact the Cag. I want the moon blocking us."

"Okay, Mark." Dan agreed.

"Ari, get Miles Jefferson on the comm."

She nodded and punched a button, then started speaking lowly. An instant later the screen at the front of the ship shimmered to life and an image of the Cagliostro's command deck appeared.

"Hey, boss." Jefferson greeted them with a forced smile.

"Miles, we're going to need you here."

"Don't know if I can help, boss. Remember that ship we did a number on, on the way here? Well it's back and it brought friends."

"What are you talking about?" Mark replied, concern suddenly written all over his face.

"That big war ship we took out is here, searching for us, and it brought two more just like it. I don't think we can get to you, at least not without getting fried out here. We're playing cat an' mouse with these guys right now."

"Listen to me, you get out of here, go to hyper-warp immediately and start heading back toward Earth. That is an order, Mr. Jefferson."

"Wait—are you kidding me? You want us to bug out and leave you here?"

"I want you to save my crew and ship. The Stargrazer is more than capable of hyper-warp interstellar flight. You can't do us any good by getting killed or getting the ship destroyed. Now do as I ask and get out of here. We'll contact you when we find what we're looking for."

"Well, how far do you want us to go?"

"Go as far as you have to lose any pursuit. I don't care if that's right back to Earth itself. Just do it and do it now. Get out of here."

Miles nodded, despair on his face, "Alright boss, whatever you say. We're outta here."

The image on the viewer faded back to a starscape and the moon they were hiding behind.

"What do we do now, Mark?" Ariel asks.

"We're going to have to go back. That's the only thing we can do."

"How can we do that?" Red barked, "They have patrols both in space and on that planet's surface looking for us. If we go back to that space port we'll be shot on sight, hell the 'Grazer will be shot down the minute we head towards a landing pad."

"Oh ye of little faith. The 'Grazer is a tough little ship, I'm less concerned with going back there then I am of escaping once we find what we're looking for. Besides, who said we were going back to any landing site?"

Chapter Seven

The Stargrazer slipped back planet-side over the most unpopulated portion of the desert world. Sliding in under security and sensor scans, before landing in a densely wooded mountain range near where Mark and the crew suspected the mysterious captive had been taken.

"Invisibility generator is off." Red affirmed.

"Good. For now the trees can cloak us. Ari, do you sense anything, or anyone?" Mark asked.

"No, but I'm hearing a mental murmur east of here. It may not be who we're looking for, there's no way of knowing until I hear thoughts I can make definite decisions on. Right now it's all just noise."

"Alright Dan, give me a hand back in the hold."

"Whatcha got?" Big Dan Sledge replied as he unbuckled himself and followed Johnson to the back of the ship.

"Well, we can't just fly around in the Stargrazer looking for our mystery man, but we can take these babies out and cover more ground a bit more inconspicuously." Mark pulled the cover off the first item he pulled out of the hold. It was a gleaming black sky-cycle, and there were three more just like it within.

"Only four?" Dan asked.

"Yes, someone stays with the ship."

"Hhhmmph, Ari's not gonna like that."

"Who said it's Ariel who is going to stay?"

"What? Me? You're gonna make me stay?"

"You're the best pilot Dan. You can have the ship out of cover and to whoever needs you in minutes."

"Yeah but I'm also the guy who can shatter brick and steel with his bare hands."

"And right now I need you for your piloting skills, not your incredible strength."

"Alright. I really don't like this one bit, but just give me a yell if ya need me."

"Believe me Danny, you'll be the first to hear."

The big man nodded somberly. Everyone exited the ship and met Dan and Mark at the back hatch where they stood there with the four sky cycles. Stylish modern machines with tires just like any other motorcycle, but also an anti-grav magno-disc built into each solid rim. Black flight suits were donned over their regular uniforms and black helmets with a blackened face shield which was actually a HUD or Heads up Display linking first to the sky cycle then to the Stargrazer itself, sharing information across vast distances.

"Search pattern delta to begin with." Mark ordered, and the four cycles suddenly leaped straight upwards, then away, disappearing into the night sky. Small horizontal wings slid out of the sides of each to aid in aerodynamics. Below, Dan Sledge shook his head in disgust and re-entered the Stargrazer, sealing the hatch behind him.

"He's not happy." Red spoke into the communicator within his helmet.

"Do you blame him? He was just left behind."

Dan's voice crackled through their headsets "I can still hear ya, ya know."

Ariel laughed, "It's okay Dan, I'm sure we'll be calling you any minute to rescue us."

"Haha," came his crackled his reply.

"All right kiddies, let's find this guy, whoever he is, and see what's really going on here."

Across his helmet's HUD Mark was watching numbers and heat signatures fly by in quick succession. He hoped the small sky cycles were invisible to the scanners used on this world. There was plenty of shielding built into them for just that purpose, but he had no way of knowing for certain.

"Okay, it's time to expand our grid," he ordered. "Eddie and Red flank right, and begin arcing back towards the 'Grazer. Ari and I will arc left. If you see anything call out immediately."

"Aye aye, skipper." Eddie replied sarcastically.

"Watch it there pal, I still sign your paychecks."

"Yeah, don't I know it."

The four sky cycles split up and rocketed through the sky.

The minutes dragged on in silence as the small sky cycles criss-crossed the sky above the designated search location.

"Anything yet?" Mark asked.

"No not yet. Nothing out here but farm animals of some kind that resemble cows."

"It's amazing that this is one of the only mountainous regions on this world." Ariel offered.

"I know, it's strange. There's actually some vegetation here as well, and yet signs of habitation are few and far between. Most of these people on this sparsely populated world tend to be near the commerce centers. It's a dust bowl, but at least they can have some form of a social life."

"It's a dreary world. That's kind of an understatement, I know, but there's not much other way to describe it." Ari replied.

"Yes I know, still there has to be something significant about it for them to drag the General here, if that is who it is."

"Do you really think they have Abruzzi here? Then who was that we've been dealing with?"

"Ari, I don't know. I know it definitely wasn't him, that much I can tell you. He may be a stodgy pain in the ass, but what he's been putting us through the past few weeks has been just shy of crazy. Whoever that is taking his place has done his best to confiscate the Cagliostro, which means we would have never made this flight. In fact I have no doubt the ship would have exploded the moment it went to hyper-warp, and that would have ended our deep space program before it started."

"Wow," she murmured, "I hadn't thought of that."

"This is a convoluted mess, Ariel, and it's only likely to get worse before we figure it all out."

"What's worse is we have no one to back us up."

Mark nodded as his sky cycle sped over treetops, "I know the Cag is gone now too. We're really on our own out here, which is definitely something that can bite us if something goes wrong."

As if in response to his last comment a spotlight suddenly shined upon him and Ariel from above, and then a voice boomed, "You will land your vehicles immediately and allow yourselves to be subject to a search. Land now. You will not be warned again."

"Yeah, I don't think so." Mark replied to his crew over the comm link and suddenly shot his sky cycle straight upwards, past their pursuers. Ariel followed but on a different vector.

"Hell, it's more of those two-man gunships that were after us at the space port." Mark grunted angrily.

"Do you two need help?" Reds voice cut through instantly.

"Yeah you could say that." Mark replied testily.

"On our way." Red confirmed.

Mark and Ariel zig-zagged their sky cycles to and fro, avoiding deadly energy beams that lanced out towards them from the two-man gunship dogging their tail.

"Watch out Ariel I'm going to try to draw their attention." Mark shouted into his microphone.

Sliding his cycle to the right of Ariel's, he flipped it over in midair, and sped across the bow of the gunship, then dove down and back up, looping around the two-man craft. When he was facing them directly he fired the two small laser blasters equipped on the sky cycle. Scoring a direct hit on the larger ship.

The problem was that the weapons on the sky cycles were small discharge blasters, and could do no real damage to the heavily armored gunships.

Now it was a dance of death over the blackened landscape with the stars twinkling overhead, as the two small sky cycles dove and spun through the night sky, avoiding the attacks of the much more heavily armed, two-man gunship, its bubble canopy showing the helmeted faces of their antagonists within.

First Mark would draw their fire, then Ariel, as each took turns blasting the larger vehicle, their energy pulses splashing off its armored hide like water.

"This is no good; we're hardly making a mark on that thing." Johnson lamented.

"I know, but we can't run, they'll shoot us down right away."

"I know Ari; we have to hold on until the others get here."

"Here now." Red's voice intruded as his sky cycle dove down between the attacking gunship and Ariel's sky cycle.

"An' he ain't alone!" Shouted Eddie as he raced his sky cycle through the air from above the attack craft, heading towards it and strafing it as he passed over it.

"I'm feeding you all the aiming coordinates. Fire there. Together we can take this thing out." Red shouted.

"Agreed." Mark replied as the bigger craft turned again and headed towards them. Each Sky Cycle split off from the others in another direction, Each time the two-man craft would draw a bead on one cycle another would attack it, spinning by it, or sliding through the air sideways above or below the small gunship, all aiming their weapons at the same spot, the side of the engine cover at the rear of the patrol vehicle.

This dance of death went on for several minutes, until at one point Ariel flew too slowly, and too close to the small gunship, when one of its blasters found its mark, tearing through the rear wheel of her sky cycle disintegrating it explosively and causing the cycle to cartwheel sideways though the sky.

"Ariel!" Mark shouted as he dove his sky cycle towards her at full throttle through the black sky. "Jump!" He shouted both mentally and verbally, praying she'd hear him one way or another.

Ariel's sky cycle continued to spin toward the treetops below, now looming much closer in the blackness. Suddenly she was flung free as instantly, Mark dove his cycle directly towards her only a heartbeat behind her decent.

The deadly impaling tree tops loomed through the darkness as Johnson, his sky cycle's engine screaming, grasped her flailing arm and pulled her up to him. Ariel immediately set herself behind Mark on the long seat and clung to him tightly. '*I'm okay,*' is all she said mentally to him.

He patted her hand and then squeezed it as he looped his sky cycle in a tight circle, as far below the Sky Cycle Ariel had been riding exploded violently when it finally hit the ground, so far below the trees.

Accelerating madly he climbed his sky cycle towards the battle being played out across his HUD. Now aiming from his far removed position from the battle he began firing upon the two-man patrol ship, concentrating his fire on the target Red had directed them to aim at.

The gunship turned towards Mark and Ariel, but was attacked from above by Eddie as Red arced around it once more and concentrated his fire on the same spot again. Now all three sky cycles attacked the engine cover and within seconds it glowed bright orange and exploded with a horrific grinding of metal. The gunship hurled itself sideways and disappeared within the trees. An instant later a muffled explosion and a burst of flame shot up from below.

"Is everybody all right?" Mark frantically shouted into his comlink.

"Yes," Eddie replied.

"Ditto," answered Red.

"What just happened there?" Ari asked.

"I think we discovered where they're hiding the General." Mark replied.

"You think we overflew where they have him stashed?" Red asked.

"Yes, I do. I don't believe that there'd be a heavily armed patrol ship in the middle of nowhere. Something's being hidden there. I'm sure it's who we're looking for."

"Now all we have to do is remember where the patrol ship came after us and start a search from there." Red commented.

"Not that difficult a thing to do," Mark explained, "all we do is recall the data going backwards to the point where the gunship attacked us, and fan out from there."

Ariel squeezed his shoulder from behind as the sky cycle zoomed low over the treetops, heading back to where they came from.

"That was pretty smart," she said with a smile, while she patted him on his shoulders playfully.

"Well Ari, you have to remember," he began, smiling wryly within his helmet, "I am a genius."

Chapter Eight

The sky cycles converged on the spot the attack had begun.

"From here we expand in a 'K' pattern, sensors on the helmets on full front, Danny, are you there?"

"Yes I am boss." Dan's voice replied over the helmet headset.

"Okay Dan, keep us on your sensors and be ready to take off at a moment's notice, we may need a quick pick up. Conversely, we may need a distraction along the way too."

"Gotcha boss." Dan replied.

The three small sky cycles spread out once again, flying low and slow over the black treetops. After twenty minutes of repeating the pattern over and over again, Eddie spoke up over the comm "I got something boss."

"You wanna share?" Red broke in.

"Yeah I have some heat signatures but they're faint. I think they might be underground, because I'm not showing anything on the surface. No buildings, no anything. Yet I'm seeing what looks like bodies moving around. I think there are tunnels down there."

"Okay, converge on Ariel and I. We're landing, and walking from here."

A minute later the three sky cycles were on the ground and all four members of the team were off and walking, each using a hand-held scanner that replicated what the Heads up Display within the helmet had done.

"I'm seeing the same heat signatures you were a few minutes ago." Mark began, " They are definitely below ground. Now we have to find their entrance. Fan out in a straight line and set your scanners to 'full sensitivity mode'. Let's find out how these people are getting below ground."

"Whatever you say Mark." Eddie agreed as he walked in an opposite direction from Mark and Ariel. Red trailed Eddie.

"What've you got Red?" The smaller man asked.

"Nothin' Eddie, nothin' yet." Red murmured, while watching his scanner.

Ariel and Mark walked side by side as two of the planets four moons shone brightly in the sky overhead. "Nice night, and at least this small oasis is a nice place to be. It's kind of romantic," she remarked.

"Hhhmm? Yes it is romantic I suppose, though I'd rather be able to take advantage of that when our lives aren't at stake." He turned and smiled at her. "And you are right it is kind of an oasis, except with more trees, and it's a good fifty mile swath of land that's like this with the small mountain range jutting out of nowhere."

"It's a little strange isn't it that this is the only piece of land anywhere around here that's built like this?"

Mark stopped, smiled, leaned forward and kissed her. "Looks like I'm not the only genius here. That was brilliant."

Ariel stared at him, perplexed. What was? What did I say?"

He laughed in a low voice, almost a whisper really, "You said 'built'. That's exactly what this place is. It's been terraformed. This fifty mile stretch of land was terraformed for a reason. Now, what is that reason? That's what we have to ascertain. Any suggestions?"

She stared wide eyed at him for a moment then looked around. "I-I have no idea," she replied, shaking her head.

"It doesn't matter, I'm sure we'll figure it out on our own soon enough. Now that I'm actually thinking about it, I'll let my subconscious work on it while we continue with the job at hand."

Ariel stared at him through slit eyes a moment, "Sometimes you really scare me," she laughed quietly.

"So, I guess I'll take that as a compliment then," he replied with a smirk of his own.

"Hey boss, Mark, do you read me?" Red's voice rumbled through the communicator.

Johnson touched his sleeve and replied, "Yes Red. Find something?"

"We did, our entrance. I'm sending the coordinates to your suits GPS. Come and meet us. And hurry. This place is guarded."

"On our way Red. ETA is four minutes."

Mark and Ariel looked at each other and began to jog through the woods as quietly as possible, the bright light reflecting off of the two moons in the sky providing ample light, even at this time of the night.

"What do you think?" Eddie didn't even look their way as they arrived. He kept his eyes locked on the target before them.

Mark and Ariel looked on from behind thick tree coverage as their scanners depicted a scene they were too far from to actually see. A concrete double doorway, seemingly going nowhere but down, with two armed guards standing silently out in front of it.

"Only two guards?" Mark turned his head towards Red and asked.

"Two that we can see on scanners and I'm sure there are more walking around out here. Plus, don't forget we were attacked in the air. I have a feeling that was just a patrol."

"Yes," Mark answered, "a patrol that didn't check back in as of yet."

"You don't think they know their men are down?" Eddie asked, incredulous.

"No. Do you see any activity here? Any men running in and out of this place? I don't see anything. Those two guards at the door are not even really paying attention to what's going on around them. They're relaxed."

"Good points, Mark." Red hissed.

"So do we charge them?" Ariel whispered.

"Why not?" Mark replied quietly.

Mark turned and looked up at Red as they were all bent low hiding in the trees shadows and foliage. "What do you think? Spread out and shoot them down?"

Red stood there a moment and then shook his head side to side in reply. "Something's not right about this. This is almost too inviting."

"You think it looks like a trap?" Ariel asked.

"Why don't you tell us Ariel?" Eddie nodded towards the double doors.

She closed her eyes and mentally reached out with her telepathy a moment. "Nothing." She spoke quietly as she opened her eyes.

"What do you mean 'nothing'?" Mark asked warily.

"I'm not reading anything. Nothing from those men. It's like they are not even there."

"Maybe they are not." A new voice intruded upon them as bright lights suddenly blazed to life about them. "Lower your weapons and you won't be harmed. Resist and we'll just take your bodies inside." A figure walked forward towards them from outside the ring of lights that now blinded them. Then his face came into focus quickly.

"You." Mark snorted as he stood up, the crew following his example.

"You're that officer, or whatever you are, who tried to take us at the spaceport. I thought we killed you?" Red asked smiling.

"Not quite." The alien replied as he fired two quick energy blasts from the pistol in his right hand into Red's chest, dropping him to the forest floor like a sack of meat.

Ariel inhaled sharply as Red's body spasmed a few times, then lay there on his back with the two holes in his chest smoldering. The alien turned sharply and ordered, "Leave him. Get the rest inside. We have to sort this all out, don't we?"

Chapter Nine

"So, somehow you survived a point blank blast from a starship's wing canon. Even set on its lowest setting you should have been killed. And yet here we are all talking to each other. This is all very interesting." Mark commented, his face set grimly.

"My existence is none of your concern, but I will tell you that was my predecessor who you killed with your ship."

Ariel turned towards Mark; he grinned slightly and almost imperceptibly nodded. She faced front again. Mark, Eddie and Ariel were seated with their hands bound before them in what could only be called an interrogation cell beneath the ground, down a long subterranean corridor that curved below the ground almost from the moment of entry at the concrete door platform above.

"You Earthmen are quite extraordinary. You muddle around on your own world for centuries and leap to worlds within your own solar system, then in no time at all, at least cosmological time that is, you suddenly decide you want to play with the big boys and join the rest of the universe. The gall of you beings. You are a minor race, nothing more. You do not deserve to be out amongst the stars with your betters. You have not matured enough yet as a race. You should not be flying amongst the stars for centuries to come. Your unmitigated gall as a species, well I find it personally appalling."

"I'll make sure to relay your message when we get home." Mark replied.

"Your sarcasm merely reinforces what I have just said, human. You are a belligerent race of little people who think to leap amongst the stars and soon after you would seek to run the whole damned universe." The purple skinned officer waved both his hands in the air as he spoke.

"You're a little overdramatic, dontcha think?" Eddie snickered.

"You find your predicament funny? What am I to do with you people? We tried to send you all off, to make you turn around. We've done everything we could to discourage you, and yet here you are. Perhaps if we send your pieces back to your home world that would serve as enough warning not to come back out of your system, what do you think?"

Mark laughed outright then as he stood up within the small cell and walked over to stand face to face with his tormentor. Nearby the guards surrounding them tensed and fingered their weapons as they watched the confrontation begin to escalate.

"I personally think, salad head, that killing us and sending our pieces back could be the very worst thing you could do for your own races survival. If you think killing us and using us as an example is going to scare humanity, you have no idea who or what you are dealing with. All you'll do is begin an interstellar war with the absolute most war-like race you have ever encountered. Man has fought man for so many centuries over everything from religion and politics to who owns what and who should be standing on which side of the street and when. Believe me, provoke us. We're just looking for a whole new races ass to kick."

"Salad head?" The alien murmured to himself in shock, looking stunned at the insult.

"All of that and that's what sticks with you?" Eddie sat back and laughed.

The alien tormentor turned towards his subordinates with their guns trained on the crewmen. "Kill them all."

Mark turned towards Ariel, "Now." She nodded and leaned forward, her eyes rolled up into her head as she furrowed her brow. Instantly the three guards and their master dropped to the ground holding their skulls and screamed in agony.

"Did you think your Quel was the only one who knew how to play mind tricks? He may have taken Ariel by surprise once, but she has no trouble using his own tricks against you. She's been doing mind assaults like this for a long time. She's more than just a mind reader; she's the most powerful telepath on my planet. Something else you can hold against us I suppose. Enjoy your pain; you'll be unconscious in a few more seconds."

As if on cue, the four aliens dropped to the ground, insensate, and shuddering. Ariel stood then, stumbled and almost fell to the ground, but Mark and Eddie jumped to her side, catching her and holding her up.

"Relax Ariel, you were fantastic as usual, leave the rest to us." Ariel nodded as a trickle of blood ran down from her nose. She sat back upon the bench as Eddie tried to get the keys off the jailors belt to their binders.

Suddenly the door at the end of the hallway exploded with a rumble that shook the whole cavern.

"Dammit, he could have waited a few more minutes." Mark fumed.

"Hey I'm glad he's coming now, at least he can help get these cuffs off." Eddie replied.

The sound of a blaster discharging echoed down the hall as the aliens could be heard scurrying between the escaping threesome and the doorway in fear, after a few more blaster bolts.

Abruptly Red appeared in their doorway, his blaster still smoking.

"Get these things off of us," Eddie yelled.

Red snorted and smiled, "In trouble without me again, huh?"

"Just help us get these cuffs off," Mark grumbled. "Ari, were you able to find him while I talked to this mook?"

Before she could reply, a vaguely familiar voice shouted from several cells further down the hall, "Who's down there? I hear perfect English, not like these morons talk. Are those earthmen I hear?"

"We don't need a translator for that, do we?" Eddie chortled.

"No, not this time." Mark replied, "General is that you? Where are you?"

"Johnson? Is that you? But how?"

They ran down the hall to the General's cell where the bedraggled, heavy set man stood holding onto the bars before him. His clothes were filthy and torn, as if he had been there for a long time in captivity.

"Stand back sir, we'll get you out of here."

"Harrumph, it's about time, too." The older man grumbled as a blaster bolt from Eddie's recovered gun

Ralph L. Angelo, Jr.

struck the lock on his cell door, obliterating it. The haggard
looking old man stumbled out of the cell on legs long
unused by his imprisonment. He had a heavy white beard,
no longer just his bushy white mustache. His hair was
unkempt, and he needed a shower, badly. But then he
smiled slightly, "I'm happy to see you clowns." He
growled as Red grabbed him and helped him to walk
towards the doorway.

"We have to get out of here. This place is going to be
teeming with guards any second." Mark commanded.

As if in response to his statement, blaster bolts started
ricocheting off the walls above their heads. Behind them
came the sound of running footsteps, followed by more
energy bolts.

"Eddie, Red, buy us some time."

"You got it boss." Eddie nodded as he un-holstered his
gun once again. He and Red ducked down on opposite
sides of the roughhewn walkway, behind jutting stones.
Eddie pointed at the light panels overhead and Red nodded.
Both men began firing at the overhead lighting, throwing
the cavernous walkway into blackness.

Heading towards them out of the blackness came a
score of men, with weapons that had glowing muzzles that
got brighter as they charged up to fire.

"Aim above the muzzles." Eddie shouted to Red above
the din of the ricocheting blaster bolts continued onslaught.

"Will do, squirt." Red replied as both men laid down a
blanket of energy bolts, strafing the cell blocks floor again
and again. Screams of injured and dying men shrieked out
from the darkness as Red and Eddie began backing up
towards the entrance.

Red touched the communicator built into his uniforms right sleeve. "Boss, get us outta here."

Outside the facility, Mark touched his uniforms communicator and replied, somewhat frantically "I'm working on it, Red," he paused a second, "Danny where are you? Now would be a good time…"

"On my way, Mark!" Dan replied as the Stargrazer banked wide overhead, turning the night sky to day with its powerful lights. The ship paused in midair then silently dropped to the ground vertically as a side door slid away, from inside Dan shouted, "Let's go! Move it!"

Johnson and Ariel raced into the ship, half dragging the General with them, a few seconds later Eddie and Red backed out of the devastated doorway below, firing back into the underground facility with every step.

"Move it!" Shouted Mark from the ships door, as he waved them in. Blaster bolts ricocheted about them as the men threw themselves into the ship. An instant later the door shut behind them as the Stargrazer was already climbing towards space.

Everyone buckled into a seat as the ship raced through the sky, ascending like a meteor in reverse.

"Look out!" Ariel shouted, pointing as two big, heavily fortified ships came into view just as they cleared the last vestiges of atmosphere and shot into the eternal darkness of the void.

"They're shootin' at us." Dan rumbled as he banked the ship hard astern, then dove down, and quickly up as it spun around and around narrowly avoiding a stream of seemingly never-ending, deadly, energy blasts.

"Get us outta here Danny!" Mark ordered through gritted teeth, as he held onto his control console.

"Whattaya think I'm tryin' ta do?" Dan replied with a shout.

"Eddie! Return fire, Now!"

"Already on it!" Eddie squawked as he fired the small ships guns again and again.

"Those ships aren't as big or as heavily shielded as that one we fought in deep space, our blasts are actually scorin' hits."

"Yeah, but Eddie, there's a lot more ship out there trying to hit us then there is here trying to hit them, so I repeat, Danny, get us out of here!" Mark yelled.

The Stargrazer screamed through space, arcing first left then right, then straight up as both bigger ships slowly turned to chase it, until with energy blasts splashing off its shields and skin, the Stargrazer suddenly flipped over and dove directly at the attacking ships, accelerating directly between them. Eddie continued to fire at them both until once alongside both ships Danny hit the hyper-warp and the Stargrazer disappeared in a splash of light.

"Those two ships will be after us in a minute." Red grunted.

"I know, Ari, try to get in touch with the Cagliostro. We need her fire power."

"Cagliwhatstro?" The General grunted "What the hell is a Cagliostro?"

"It's my ship." Mark replied.

"Is that what you named her? Why the hell would you name that bird such a stupid name?" The old General laughed.

Mark turned on the old man, annoyed, "It was the name of a sixteenth century alchemist and sorcerer. No one believed he could do what he claimed, just like none of you believed the Cag would break the light speed barrier. But guess what, you old pain in the ass, the Cagliostro not only broke the light speed barrier, it obliterated it. That ship, and this one as well, by the way, isn't only faster than light, its thousands of times faster. And if not for me and that ship you'd be living out what's left of your life in a cell on that dustbowl of a planet." Mark finished.

The General looked at him with vehemence; steam was practically coming out of his ears. But then he suddenly softened and looked away, not wanting to match his eyes to Marks. "You're right son, I do owe you my life. Without you and your ship I'd have died there. I'm sorry." He raised his eyes finally and met Mark's, "I have a feeling this whole adventure is far from over too. I think we may have a long way to go. I also know I'm not the only one who owes you. The whole damned planet will if you can pull this off. You're literally going to save the world."

"Thanks for the vote of confidence; General, but we're a very long way from home." Mark turned toward Ariel, "Any word from the Cag yet?"

"Nothing Mark. Not a peep. I'm looping the hail, and hoping it gets through to them as we get closer."

"Red, what about our company back there?"

"I see them, but they're not gaining on us."

"Alright, Danny don't spare the horses, full throttle and keep it pinned."

"I'm doing that now Mark, but honestly, we're running an untested ship here, and I have no idea how long we can keep her going all out."

"I do, I designed this ship and its engines. I know what it can handle, even if the specs don't show it. We can handle it. We have to. We got lucky back there. If those two big bruisers catch us, we'll be done for."

Chapter Ten

"I think they're gone." Mark announced, as he turned and faced Ariel, who sat next to him.

For eight long hours the chase had continued, with the Stargrazer running its engines full out, overrunning the specs they were designed for, just to ensure the crews survival.

Ariel nodded, and smiled slightly, "Thank God we lost them. That was getting to be tedious."

"I don't know if I would have termed it that way, but yes, I get your meaning." Mark replied and relaxed a bit in his chair.

"How'd you know?" Ariel asked Mark, who sat at the ships controls flying the Stargrazer while Danny took a few minutes rest.

"Hhmm? How'd I know what?"

"That Red was alive. You weren't the least bit surprised when he came bursting in guns blazing."

"Eight hours later and now you ask me this? That's easy. The suits we're all wearing. I told you they were bullet and blaster proof, at least to small weapons fire."

"What about the burning holes I saw after he got hit?"

"That's how the uniforms work. They convert energy and displace it. It's all part of the design. With bullets it's a matter of converting the kinetic energy, with blasters it's displacing the energy and shunting it off. It's a great system."

"Okay I get that now, but what about that alien boss back there, he said the guy we shot with the Stargrazer's gun was his 'predecessor'. What did that mean?"

"Yes what did that mean?" The General asked as he entered the cabin from the sleep quarters in the back.

"Not sleeping General? I'm surprised."

"Believe me, son, I've gotten enough rest the past few months in that hell hole. I didn't mean to eavesdrop, but I heard you talking about that little gestapo wannabe. What was that about?"

Mark grinned and took a deep breath, "He was a clone. So is your replacement by the way."

"What? What are you talking about? They cloned me? When?"

"Probably months ago, maybe longer. All they needed was a stray hair or some skin follicles. They made another you, without a mind of course, and programmed him to do their bidding. That's how they were hoping to stall us, and stop my FTL drive from ever being completed."

The General sat back in his seat, looking stunned. "Bastards," was all he said.

"What was all that with the terraforming about?" Eddie asked as he entered the control cabin.

"Think about it, what did that mountain range look like to you? At least a small section of."

"I don't know." Ariel answered.

"Virginia."

"Huh?" Eddie barked.

"Virginia. The Blue Ridge Mountains, west of the seat of our government. They recreated the Blue Ridge Mountains and built a base under them. Guaranteed that same base is under the real Blue Ridge and has been there for a long time. Far enough from DC to avoid detection, unless it's under close scrutiny, but there's been no reason for that, and close enough to feed the fake General orders and for him to have a place to report to only a short distance away."

"My God, we've been infiltrated." Abruzzi groaned.

"It's worse than that General, if they replaced you this was just the tip of the iceberg. They could very easily have replaced the President, the joint chiefs, congress, anyone. This was a carefully orchestrated assault that took years to implement. That means they have been watching us for a very long time."

"But who are "they"? Surely not the inhabitants of that backwater world."

"No, I don't believe it was anyone commanding their forces out of that dust bowl either, General. Somewhere else out there, very well hidden, is our enemy, our *true* enemy. We have to get back home, and begin retrofitting the fleet with my magno-disc engines but only after we find how deep our doppelganger problem is.

You were right before General, when you said this adventure is far from over. We have a lot ahead of us yet."

"So what now? Red asked as he rejoined everyone and slid into one of the control seats.

"Find the Cag, that's where we have to start."

"Uh, I think we just did that." Ariel turned in surprise to face Mark. She touched a control on her virtual panel and suddenly the display screen zoomed in and showed an image of the Cagliostro, listing sideways in space, motionless and dead, smoke trailing into space from her hull.

Chapter Eleven

"What the hell…" Mark rumbled.

"What do you think happened here?" Red asked Mark.

"No idea, maybe they were overrun by enemy forces. I could see the Cag holding its own and beating one of those big war ships, but against two or three?" He left the question hanging pregnant in the air.

"You think that's what happened?" Ariel asked.

"See the scarring along the hull?

She nodded in the affirmative, her face stern.

"The Cag was in a battle, and a prolonged one too, against several ships. Are you getting any life signs?" Mark turned and asked Red.

"Looking now. Doing a scan. Nothing so far, also no power anywhere on the ship it's completely out."

By now the Stargrazer had slowed out of hyper-warp and slowly pulled up near the much larger ship.

"She doesn't appear damaged, Mark, not badly at any rate, just powerless."

"When we first battled that war ship as we were heading to the sand planet, they hit us with something that drained our power and energy stores. Multiple hits of that from multiple ships would have drained her dry."

"We have to get inside." Red growled.

"What's going on?"

Everyone turned to find Danny standing in the doorway, rubbing his head dry with a towel. Then he stopped as he saw the view screen and cursed almost silently.

Dan slid into his chair and Mark returned navigation control to him. "Line up our belly hatch with the side of the Cag right there." He pointed at a spot as Dan slowly guided the smaller ship up to the side of the much larger one. The Stargrazer turned sideways and floated in, securely bumping into the side of the Cagliostro.

"Magnetic locks activated." Dan called out.

Mark was out of his seat in an instant and walking towards the center of the small spacecraft. Then he changed his footing to the wall of the ship standing on it and activating the irising portal that was on the floor of the Stargrazer.

The portal irised open and revealed the blank wall, which was actually a hatch on the outer hull of the Cagliostro. Mark picked up a heavy cable from a supply outlet on the Stargrazer and began to attach it to a mating port on the side of the door on the Cagliostro. Dan walked over and joined Mark. He took the heavy cable from Mark's hands and finished the attachment, twisting the cable until it snapped into place.

"All set." Dan nodded at Mark.

"Good. Ariel, begin power transfer." Mark called to the front of the 'Grazer. The General walked over to join them.

"Do you men need any help?"

"When we get aboard we're going to have to go through ten decks one at a time to make sure we didn't pick up any passengers, so yeah, you'll be needed General. Grab a gun and sit tight for a minute or two more."

Mark tapped a staccato pattern on a flat keypad under the same cover that the power conduits inlet was hiding beneath. After a second a retina scan read his eyes, and a DNA scan read his hand. One final code was introduced on the flush keypad and then the door slid open with power supplied by the Stargrazer.

Within the Cagliostro was darkness. Mark tapped out a pattern on the sleeve of his uniform and immediately his sleeve produced a beam of light that cut through the darkness.

The General snorted, "Too bad you couldn't make that thing into a weapon."

Mark turned to him and smiled grimly, "Who said I couldn't? Problem is too many men would blow their hands off if I did. I would probably forget from time to time myself."

The old man nodded grimly in agreement, "Valid point."

"So do we all go? Does someone stay with the 'Grazer? How do you want to play this?" Eddie asked.

Mark Johnson did not answer immediately as he read one of the small handheld scanners they had used earlier on the planet itself. "Atmosphere reads normal. Eddie, you stay here. Close the hatch behind us and be ready to open that hatch at a moment's notice if we come running."

"You think there may be some surprises left for us?"

"I wouldn't doubt it, but you never know. I'm probably just being overly cautious, which in this case is not such a bad thing. When we make it to the command deck, I'll power up the magno-discs again and restore power to the ship. Once that's done we'll open the docking bays and you can get the Stargrazer back onboard. In the meantime, hang tight."

"Sounds like a plan, boss."

"All right, General Abruzzi, Dan, Red, and Ariel with me. Ariel are you okay enough to scan for survivors mentally as well as linking us? I know you took a beating these past few days, but I have to rely on you hon, I'm sorry."

She smiled as she looked at him, "I'm fine, don't 'Mother Hen' me. I'm really okay, I'm not just saying it, I promise."

He leaned forward and kissed her quickly. They both smiled before turning and walking into the ship, flashlight beams from their uniforms sleeves were brightly illuminating the corridor they walked through. Everyone had taken a pistol before they left the Stargrazer, including the General. They all walked with their pistols drawn and ready now through the pervading darkness.

Nothing stirred.

Red took point as they walked, Dan stayed at his shoulder scanning right while Red looked left. They looked at each other and shrugged, then made a right turn down a corridor that led to the command deck.

By now enough power had been drawn from the Stargrazer to operate doors and minor systems before restarting the magno-discs. As they approached the maglovator doors to the command deck they slowly slid open. As with the rest of the ship so far, the command deck was empty.

"They fought to the very end here." Red commented while he was looking at blaster burn marks along the walls and ceiling.

"Yes, but gratefully I don't see any bodies left behind." Mark replied as he seated himself in the Captain's chair. Dan sat down in the engineers' seat and began touching virtual controls that dimly sprang to life before him.

"It's amazing they even drained the emergency energy storage cells with that weapon of theirs. If not for the Stargrazer being hooked up to us, we wouldn't even have power for the control interfaces."

"I know Dan, and I purposely gave those their own power supplies when I designed this ship."

"Let's try a re-start; we should be able to do it now. It'll be just like jumpstarting a car, with the 'Grazer attached." Dan replied.

Mark touched his sleeve, "Eddie, do you copy? We're going to restart. Be prepared."

"Will do, boss," came his crisp reply.

Sledge touched a few buttons on his slightly brighter glowing control panel and suddenly there was a slight rumble as the great ship flared to life about them.

Instantly everything came online as the magno-discs powered up and began supplying energy to all the systems.

"Air filtration and life support back online." Dan advised.

"Which brings up another curious point," Mark noticed, "The air in here was not stale. This couldn't have happened too long ago."

Dan and Red both nodded in agreement.

"Eddie," Mark spoke, "disconnect the Stargrazer from the Cagliostro and proceed to the docking bay."

"On my way, boss." Eddie's voice replied clearly.

"Red, you and General Abruzzi start making a deck by deck sweep of the ship. Holler the instant you see anything out of the ordinary."

"Danny get down to engineering and make sure everything there is okay. I felt a small rumble when the magno-discs kicked in. Let's make sure everything is still aligned properly. If you need help, I'll be there immediately."

"Eddie, when you get back on board make your way directly to the command deck, I want to go over weapons command with you to make sure everything is okay here as well."

They all agreed and within a few seconds only Ariel and Mark were left aboard the command deck.

"What do you think happened to our people?" She asked quietly while staring straight ahead.

"Whoever did this took them. That's what you and I are going to work on right now. Access the command deck's cameras and begin displaying content from about twenty four hours ago."

She nodded and touched a few controls. Upon the main view screen a video of the command deck began to play.

"Nothing there." He fingered his chin and the stubble that had grown upon it the last few days. "Move ahead two hours."

Silently she complied.

"Still nothing." He remarked after a few minutes. "Move ahead two more hours, please." Ariel nodded silently and did so. This happened several more times until finally at the ten hour mark they discovered the command deck had been in a state of bedlam.

They both watched silently as the secondary command deck crew fired weapons against enemies displayed upon the view screen as four of the same war ships that had attacked the Cagliostro previously.

"Every time they hit us, our power reserves were emptied." Mark spoke quietly. "How long did this go on for?"

"Recordings stopped about six hours ago." Ariel answered.

"So all power reserves were run dry by then. That means they fought for four hours against four ships. They must have put up a helluva fight," he remarked grimly.

Eddie exited the maglovator then and quietly took his seat at his weapons console.

"Everything okay, Eddie?"

"Yes boss, at least as good as could be expected considerin'. The Stargrazer is secured and clamped to the landing deck floor. I also checked on the shuttles they're locked in place as well. They were never touched."

"All right, thanks for the information. Go over your weapons console. We need to be prepared for these aliens when we encounter them again."

"What are you going to do about that energy draining ray or weapon or whatever it is?" Ariel asked.

"I'm going to study what information the sensors were able to gather on it as well as the video of its use and come up with a counter measure."

"Just like that?"

"Yes Ariel, just like that."

"Pretty sure of yourself again aren't you? We are out in the great unknown out here."

"Yes sweetheart, I am sure of myself, I have to be. I have to be damned sure of myself because everyone's life depends on me now."

"I wonder where they took our crew?" Eddie asked.

"We'll find out. The external sensors should have been able to pick up a hyper-warp trail from our friends out there. That should have been done before the fighting even started. If we can find that trail we can follow them right where we need to go."

Ariel swiveled her seat to face him, "You have this all figured out don't you? Aren't you worried about ever being wrong?"

"I was wrong already, Ari. Look about you for the wreckage I left behind by being so wrong."

She hesitated then and sat up taller in her seat, pushing against the back of it, "Mark I didn't mean anything- I- I, This isn't your fault," she stammered out finally.

He sighed and slumped slightly in his chair, "Ari, of course it's my fault. These people weren't military people. Most were scientists and engineers with a small security detail. If my people are dead it's all my fault. I shouldn't have agreed to do this."

"Boss," Red's voice, uncharacteristically hollow and distant came over the internal comm system, "You better get down to the gymnasium."

Just by the tone of Red's voice Mark knew it was bad. He ran from the command deck and into the maglovator, which sped him to the recreation deck. As the doors opened he smelled the stench of death. He knew what he was running to face before he even saw it, and he despaired.

The doors to the gymnasium slid open as he approached and he found Red staring at him, while the General looked away, his face a mask of solemn resolve.

Along the walls of the basketball court that comprised this section of the gymnasium were hanging the bodies of forty people. All tortured, all dead. And there, hanging at the foremost spot was the body of Miles Jefferson, his second team commander. Mark sank to his knees; his vision swam as despair washed over him, followed by blackness.

Chapter Twelve

Mark Johnson sat in the commissary of the Cagliostro. There was no one else in the room with him. He was drinking bourbon straight up, in an almost pitch black room staring at a view screen that showed empty space. Normally it piped in an image of the ship at hyper-warp. Now everything was still and unmoving on the view screen. Nothing moved. Not anything in the view screen, not even the Cagliostro itself.

The lights suddenly went to full brightness in the room. Annoyed he covered his eyes. "Shut those damned lights off, and then leave. I told you all I wanted to be left alone."

"No. I don't care what you told us. We're almost a million light years from home, and our Captain and boss is nowhere to be seen. He's in here hiding and sulking."

Mark turned towards the sound of the voice behind him, anger oozing from his pores. "Dammit Ariel! I caused the death of forty people because I had to be out here playing Captain Kirk or Flash Gordon or whoever. It's my fault they're all dead. They were not soldiers. They were all civilians, just a bunch of regular guys."

"And every one of them knew what they were getting into. You gave everyone on the ship a chance to get off before we left Earth. Those that were afraid did. The rest took their chances and were brave souls who wanted an adventure. Now, like I told you before, there are over sixty people being held somewhere. We are their only chance of survival. So get it together, mister." She smacked him on the back of the head as she finished. He turned towards her angrily, and then shook his head.

"I'm not abandoning them, Ari; I've been sitting here trying to work out a defense to that energy draining ray they used on us. I've been going over that data for two days while we did repairs on the ship. Even the General is getting his hands dirty helping out Dan. I haven't given up, not at all. But we have to defeat that power draining device they have, whatever it is before we go after them."

"Well how long are you going to wait? My God those people have been in some enemy's hands, and we don't even know who they are. We can't just sit here and do nothing."

He stood up and stared at Ariel, "What would you like us to do? Just go in guns blazing, hoping we take them out before they destroy us? That's not going to work."

"What do you think will?" She asked, looking straight into his eyes, her expression neutral.

"Here's what happens when that energy siphon, which is what I'm calling it by the way, hits us. It establishes a connection through that energy beam through the ship's hull and drains our energy stores. I believe it acts like a sort of heat sink, just siphoning, in this case, our energy level away."

"So what happens to that energy? Is it just shunted off into space? Or are they storing it somewhere and re-powering their weapons with it?" Asked Dan Sledge as he walked in the sliding doors of the commissary and sat down with Mark and Ariel.

"You tell me Danny. What do you think? My best guess is they are storing it and re-using it against us."

"I did see a power fluctuation when I was scanning them as they attacked us with it the first time."

"Yes, but it just punched through our shields like they weren't there. So how do we shield ourselves from that?" Ariel asked.

"How about we don't?" Mark replied, smiling suddenly.

"What do you mean, boss?" Dan reacted, while Ariel looked on with a confused look on her face.

"What if we could generate enough energy to keep us protected from their draining effects by overloading their system?"

"What?" Dan asked.

"Think Danny, You're a trained engineer and brilliant at what you do. Now, when they depowered the Cag they used three, maybe four ships with that siphon ray being broadcast from each of them. If we come upon them we have to be able to withstand that. One ship, maybe two, I'm not that concerned with. I think we can destroy them if we have to. We have the firepower. But it's the energy siphon that's going to be our weakness against these guys."

"So what are you thinkin'? Don't leave me in suspense."

"I'm thinking we take a page from their book and use it against them."

"What? You want to siphon their power? With only a handful of us I don't think we could come up with the tech fast enough to do that. We'd need a full crew in the machine shop and science labs."

111

"No Danny," Mark began smiling, "that's not what I meant. They used more than one ship against us, we'll do the same to them, but they won't know it."

"Huh? How? We don't have any invisibility device onboard, unless you're not tellin' me everything."

"Nope, not what I meant. Now listen closely, this is what we're going to do."

Chapter Thirteen

The Cagliostro hurtled through space, on the trail of their enigmatic foes. All six people aboard the ship were now on the command deck, including General Abruzzi.

"All systems are restored and operating at one hundred percent efficiency, Mark."

"All right Dan, thank you. Good job, by the way."

Sledge laughed from behind his console and display, "What're you thankin' me for? You did half the work."

"And I couldn't have gotten it done without you Dan, so once again, thank you." Mark answered stoically before turning toward Red, "How are we doing Red? Is the trail still there?"

"Yes the ion component of their engines energy signature is easily readable, Mark. It's glowin' like a beacon to the sensors."

"How long till we intercept them?"

"Hard to tell Mark, we can't see that far ahead with the sensors, but I'm trying to recalibrate them for that energy signature and not much else."

"Do what you can Red. If you need help, let me know I designed the damned things, I know how to mess with them better than anyone.

"I'll help ya out Red. I know those systems, an' I am the ships engineer." Dan offered.

Ariel looked at Mark cautiously then turned back to the main viewer, stoically.

"Dan, our speed?"

"One hundred percent of hyper-warp capability Mark. We can't get an iota more speed out of her."

"Dan, how are the engines holding up? I mean at this velocity?"

"So far no problems, boss, but that doesn't mean they can do this indefinitely."

"They don't have to. All they have to do is maintain this speed until we overtake our enemies."

Ariel swiveled her chair around and faced Mark, "How do you know they can't get away from us? These beings have been flying through space, deep space for who knows how long? I'd guess thousands of years. What makes you think we can catch them? And once we do, then what? They defeated this ship once already, what makes you think they can't do it again?"

"Because Ariel, Mark began, uncharacteristically grimly, "I wasn't in command."

The hours drained by interminably as the command crew sat restlessly, watching the main viewer.

"Eddie, we need coffee up here. Do me a favor and get us each a cup from the commissary. You'll have to make a fresh pot."

"No problem, chief." Eddie replied with a lopsided grin. "Just don't forget me if you find somethin'; that needs to be shot."

"I wouldn't dream of it, Eddie. When we find those ships, and our people, you're the only person I want behind the trigger of the Cagliostro's guns."

Eddie nodded and smiled, "Okay Mark I got it. Be right back."

"Hey Mark, can I talk to you a minute?" Danny stood up.

"Uh, who's flying the ship?" Red asked.

"Auto pilot, following the trail. It's all fine." Dan replied as he walked towards the maglovator. "C'mon boss, I need a word."

Mark rose from his seat, "Ari keep an eye on things?"

"There are six people on the ship and everyone except Eddie is right here," she replied.

"All right," he agreed with annoyance, "just make sure we're flying straight and you don't hear anything over your comm console."

Mark joined Dan as the doors shut behind them.

"What?" Mark asked, annoyed, and showing it.

Dan halted the maglovator before it went anywhere.

"We need to talk."

"We're doing that now. What is it?"

"You're pushing, badly, man. You have to stop. It doesn't even sound like you talking up there." Dan jerked his thumb towards the command deck.

"It's me, you know that."

"Obviously Mark, but you sure ain't actin' like yourself. What's goin' on here?"

"You know what's going on. We've had this conversation before."

"I thought you went all through that with Ari? C'mon man, you have to be yourself."

Mark turned and looked Dan directly in the eyes, "I am myself, more than ever, trust me buddy, and I know what I'm doing."

"I do trust you, definitely. I just wanna make sure you're straight in the head with this. It's us against maybe an army."

"Dan, I know what I'm doing. Believe me."

"See? This is what I'm worried about. You're not even really listenin' to me. You're 'yessin' me an' ignorin' me at the same time. What is wrong with you?" Dan asked wide eyed.

"Listen to me Danny; I was taking this whole thing too lightly. I got so caught up in the adventure, the thrill of going where no one had gone before. It was amazing stuff. Who wouldn't be? But for once the General was right about something, hell," He cocked his head sideways and smirked, "I'm sure he's been right about a lot of things in his military career, otherwise he wouldn't have gotten where he is now. The man is a professional soldier, and that's what I was missing when we took off, the right attitude. The business-like attitude to do what had to be done, no matter what it takes."

"What are you talking about, man? You took out one of those star ships that attacked us."

"No Danny, you're wrong. I didn't take it out, I damaged it. If I had been a soldier, a man like Abruzzi is, I'd have destroyed that ship and sent a message."

"Mark you can't think like that man."

"No Danny, I have to think like that, exactly like that. We were attacked and they would have killed us all, and we know that for a fact now, because of the message they sent and left just for me. Message received. Clearly. If I had thought like that forty people, whose names I know personally would still be alive. Hell, Danny, there's another sixty out there who may be dead already too. This stopped being a game and just became deadly serious. In fact it always was, and it's my fault for not treating it that way to begin with." He exhaled and started the maglovator returning to the command deck, then turned back toward Dan, "I knew what we were getting into and I treated it like a video game instead of what it was. I have to not only avenge the people who were killed because of my own foolishness, I have to save the ones who may still be alive, and heaven help those monsters who have them, because if they are hurt, these aliens are truly going to find out what this ship can do."

The maglovator doors opened and the two men walked back to their stations, Dan eyed Mark silently.

Ariel looked first to Mark, then to Dan, yet said nothing. Sitting in a chair at the back of the deck, General Abruzzi creased his brow as he folded his arms across his barrel chest and exhaled thoughtfully.

Suddenly an alert siren blared to life, then quieted to a less jarring volume within five seconds. "We've got contact, Mark." Red advised. "One ship, currently one hundred million miles ahead of us and losing ground quickly."

"Slow down to match speed to theirs. I want to be on the outskirts of our sensor range."

"Roger, Mark." Dan confirmed.

"Eddie prepare all weapons. When we do intercept them I want it to be done quickly. Also we're going to have to be ready to go on there and get our people back from them."

"What if they already dropped our people off somewhere?"

"Then Red, we'll find out where they are before we destroy that ship."

"Sounds like a plan." Red agreed.

"How do you want to do this?" Eddie asked.

"Very simply Eddie, hard and fast. Keep all solar cannons at full power and fire tight beams. I want to punch holes in their shields and then their hull."

The General smiled silently, in his seat behind Mark.

"Red, can you pick up any of the uniform tags?"

"No, nothing yet, we are pretty far off though."

"What's this 'tag', Johnson?" the general asked.

"The uniforms we all wear have various properties built into them. They can protect against small arms fire as well as energy resistance to anything short of a heavy energy rifle. They also have a locator transponder built into them, as well as a communicator in the sleeve."

"So these tags as you called them are broadcasting a signal all the time?"

"No general, it's a passive system, meaning we have to scan for them. If you don't know what to scan for, you'll never find it."

"Ingenious, but it must be limited to the range of your ships sensors then?"

"Yes, but these sensors are the best built on Earth."

The General smiled, "And since you said that son, I believe it, knowing the magic you can engineer."

"Thanks General, I think that's the nicest thing you've ever said to me." Mark smiled without looking behind him where the General was sitting.

"Well don't get used to it. I wouldn't want to ruin my reputation," the General replied with a smirk.

"You two lovebirds can stop your mutual admiration society," Red broke in, "that ship's starting to slow down."

"Danny, Eddie, are we ready for action?"

"Yeah, chief, we are. As ready as we're ever gonna be I think."

"Do they know we're here Red?"

"I don't think so, Mark. It's not what they slowed down for."

"What'd they slow down for then?"

"That." Answered Red as he brought up an image on his display, an image of a sprawling space station, a great wheel spinning slowly, majestically in space.

"Wow." Dan exclaimed, "That's some piece o' Engineerin'.

"Yes, it is, Danny. Okay we have to stop that ship from docking with it."

"I think we should get out of here," Red announced.

"Why?"

"I'm counting thirty eight ships exactly the same as the one we're following that are docked there."

"That ain't good," Eddie replied.

"Dammit!" Mark punched the arm of his chair angrily, "I'm not leaving our crew in these creature's hands."

Ariel turned towards Mark and began to speak, her voice loud, "We may not have a choice. There are thirty eight ships there. How can we even hope to take them all on?"

"I want that one. That ship."

"We don't even know if that's the one that took our people." She countered.

"It is, logically it has to be. It waited around the longest. The Cag's engines may have been powerless, but the sensor system still retained the barest amount of energy in its own emergency back-up battery pack. We all know three ships left from the video replays, and one remained. That one." He stood up and pointed from his chair at the view screen, "If they don't have our people anymore, they know where they are."

"Mark," Red began, "we've been following this ship for days now. But we've always been at least a day behind them. They could have dropped our people off anywhere along the way before we caught them."

As if in reply to Red's comment, a small alert began to blink and buzz on his own virtual display.

"Ummm, okay, scratch I said that. That's the 'Tags' being read by our sensors. That ship was shielded but that space station not so much. Sixty tags just appeared." He turned back to face Mark, "You were right boss, they're all here."

"Not for long."

"Johnson," The General began, "You can't really be thinking of taking that thing on can you?"

"I thought you of all people would be behind me here, General."

"I don't believe in fighting losing wars, son. There's no way you can win here and save your people."

"I disagree with you, General. I'm just working out the kinks of all this right now." Mark sat back and rubbed his chin pensively.

'I hate when you look like that,' Ariel commented telepathically.

'Why is that?' Mark replied.

'Because it usually means trouble that leaves me questioning why I started dating you.'

He looked at her and grinned boyishly, *'Probably more for my looks then my brains.'*

'Actually it was probably more for your money.' she smiled gently back at him.

"Well? Are you two going to stop the mental love making so we can get back to what's at hand?" Eddie cut in.

"Already back on it, Eddie. Just crunching the numbers, and seeing where things are going to land."

Mark leaned forward in his chair then, "Red, where are our crew, can you pinpoint them?"

The view screen changed to a grid type pattern before their eyes, blotting out the view of space and the station. Then it zoomed in and overlaid a schematic type diagram of the station itself. "This appears to be a subsection of the station that I have to assume is a jail. There are what I would call cells here, and in six of those cells are our people."

"So ten to a cell, nice, jam them together, very hospitable of these aliens."

"How close are they to the ships that are docked?" Dan asked.

"The ships are docked along the outer rim of the wheel of this station. The crew is being kept at the hub, it seems most of the population is at the hub. The 'spokes' of this wheel are tubes they use to travel to and from the ships docking ports. The outer part of the wheel seems to be maintenance areas as well as defenses and the docking ports themselves." Red finished.

"This gets worse and worse," Eddie commented, and shook his head disgustedly.

"Not really, the problem just changed, that's all Eddie. They are keeping everyone together, at least for now, and that's a major plus for us."

"So what are we going to do? We can't just charge in there, guns blazing, to use your own terms. We'll be annihilated."

"You're right Eddie. But we still have to get our people back."

"So what are you thinkin'?"

"Bait and switch."

Everyone turned towards the General sitting behind them on the Cag's command deck.

"What are you suggesting, General?" Mark asked.

"You draw them off, while some of us go onto the station as close to our people as possible and free them."

"How do you expect to pull that off?"

"Your other ship, the smaller one."

"The Stargrazer? What are you talking about?"

"Listen Johnson, you make a run at them with this bird, while the Stargrazer sits hidden behind a moon in stationary orbit, like you did earlier. Then when all their attention is on this ship and they leave to chase it, you have someone go in with the Stargrazer, punch a hole in their hull and get our people out."

"Wait," Eddie began, "You want to stuff sixty people into the Stargrazer? They'd be packed in there like Sardines."

"Maybe so, but who'd notice they were gone with all the mayhem this ship would be causing?"

"That's a valid point, General, but we'd have to work out shield generator emplacements on the station as well as the ships."

"No Mark," Dan interrupted, "We'd need to work out where their engines were the most vulnerable."

"What're you thinking Danny?"

"We wound as many ships as possible as quickly as possible, in as many ways as possible. Get the number of ships cut down as far as we can, then hightail it out of there. The remainder will be chasing us, hopefully and leave the Grazer free to attach itself to their hull near the cells. We cut through the hull grab our people and hyper-warp out of there to meet up with the Cagliostro at a pre-determined place."

Mark turned towards Abruzzi, "What do you think, General, it was your idea?"

"I think it's a solid plan. I also think we'll need some luck on our side."

"Red? You're my security man, what are your thoughts?"

The burly security chief shook his head with downcast eyes and then looked up at his boss. "I really can't think of a better idea. I think it'll work. The Cag is heavily shielded, and if they try their power draining weapon with the modifications we came up with, I think we should be able to handle them."

Dan Sledge nodded in agreement, "Even without the 'Grazer here, we'll be fine if they hit us with that thing again."

"Only thing that remains is who goes with what ship?"

"I'm staying with you, wherever that is." Ariel demanded.

"Son, I have a suggestion as far as your teams go. Your two big men and the sharp shooter have to go rescue those civilians. Being that your pilot is super humanly strong and fairly invulnerable will make him plenty useful in that raid. The born warrior with the red hair will be very helpful in that firefight and the marksman is a necessity. That leaves you, me, and your girlfriend as the crew here. That's my recommendations, as a military man I think that's the best plan."

Mark nodded slowly and began to grin slightly, "I'm learning more from you every hour, General."

"Ha! I'm just a bull headed old fool who has seen a few missions under fire, son. I picked up a few things along the way, that's all."

"All right. Let's get this show on the road. We need a technical scan of one of those ships."

Red touched a virtual button and a display went up before Mark and Dan on their consoles, "Already done when we were following that behemoth in."

"Good man, Red. Now we have to look over their engine design for flaws and weaknesses while the rest of us get ready."

"You do know we have a better chance of being blown away then we do of succeeding, right boss?" Eddie asked.

"Yes Eddie, I do, just as well as you do, but we have no choice in the matter. Too much is riding on this."

"What about the people back home?" Ariel asked.

"The Earth is safe, Ariel. There are almost two hundred destroyer class war ships between the outer edge of the solar system and Earth."

"Only problem there, Mark, is the General's clone," she replied.

"Which only means we have to get back to Earth before any of these ships do."

"Once we attack, and they realize who we are, you know they are definitely going to make a beeline towards Earth," Red commented.

"Yes I do, Red, so that just means we'll have to beat them there."

"Don't worry boss, I know this will work." Dan acknowledged.

"You're more confident than I am, Danny." Mark turned and looked about the command deck, then smiled like a predator, "Let's get moving. It's time to go hunting."

Chapter Fourteen

The Cagliostro dropped out of hyper-warp directly in front of the space station, so quickly that no one on board had time to react. The ship streaked around the huge wheel in space, firing all its weaponry at different ships docked at its huge hull.

Missiles, as well as energy blasts, leaped from the manta ray shaped starship, every weapon was precisely aimed, and all found their mark. Within two minutes, thirty five ships had damaged engines or shield generators. The cannons aboard the space station glowed brightly, their energy discharges began to come closer and closer to finding their mark as they explosively seared space all about the Cagliostro, which under Mark's deft hand flipped and spun through space, diving and ascending rapidly.

Then the Cagliostro suddenly flipped over and reversed direction in mid-course and sped away, disappearing into hyper- warp. Instants later the remaining three ships that were undamaged were in pursuit, also disappearing after their prey in explosive barrages of light.

That was when the true mission began.

The Stargrazer dropped out of hyper-warp, literally on the bottom of the station. The flash of hyper-warp curtain being dropped should have been unseen by anyone, who would have been more concerned with the damage the station and the ships docked to it had just been subject too.

The Stargrazer attached itself via its magnetic belly hatch as a hole was quickly and quietly cut into the hull of the station itself and Dan, Red and Eddie advanced quickly to the prison level.

"So far, so good," Red whispered.

"Yeah, don't jinx it," Dan growled almost imperceptibly.

"I got movement heading our way," Eddie advised while looking at his handheld scanner.

All three men wore armored suits now with see though helmets. Like their regular uniforms, the armor was blue and white.

Eddie ducked low and peered around a door edge as several blasts of light seared the walls above his head. He looked up and gulped hard before returning fire.

Now it was a pitched fire fight between three men and an army.

Red looked down at the scanner in his hands, "Our people are behind them. We have to get through these guys before we can go any further."

"Yeah leave that to me, you two keep firin'" Dan ordered as he ran into the hallway, suddenly taking two huge, bounding steps then hurling his armored form into the amassed troops with a loud 'Boom!'

Even as Dan cleared the enemies out of the way, another wave of the stations guards came rushing down the hallway at him. As he braced himself for their assault, a blast of energy flew past him and exploded into the converging guards, scattering them like leaves in a hurricane.

Dan spun around and saw Red standing there in his armored suit holding what could only be described as a small cannon. It hung from a strap over his shoulder and the end was still smoking as Red grinned behind his plexi-steel face mask. "Mark VII energy canon. Perfect for crowd dispersal."

"You're tellin' me?" Dan replied as he turned back and began running to the cells.

Eddie had set up where they had cut the hole in the floor with a tripod mounted energy rifle. He looked at his scanner as Red did the same.

"We got incomin' Red."

"I know, slick. You ready?"

DiGenovese smiled and snapped his head sideways for half a heartbeat then back upright. "Mamma DiGenovese didn't bring up a boy who wasn't."

"I pity yer mamma." Red grumbled, as he wrapped the strap to the handheld cannon tightly in his right hand.

Behind them, along the sides of the hallway, Dan Sledge raised both his powerful hands above his head and brought them crashing down upon the force field holding the crew within the cells so powerfully the floor shook and those within the cell were knocked off their feet. Despite all his might though, nothing happened.

"Uh-oh." Sledge remarked

An auburn haired beauty ran to the bars out of the crowd of blue and silver suited captives. "Nothing can take that field down. We think it's a kinetic energy field."

"Scientists," Dan grumbled disdainfully under his breath, "Get back Reynolds," he addressed her," This is gonna make a mess."

Sledge walked away from the force field, to the wall next to it where its controls were mounted. He stood against the opposite wall then charged the one he was facing, head down, like a maddened bull. The wall shattered into dust and crumbling debris as he charged through it. A half second later his fists tore through the wall of the cell, shredding the stone and steel cell like tissue paper.

"Ever'body out!" He roared. "Head down to Eddie and Red, they gotcha covered. Go!"

He repeated the same actions with the cells next to the first one and within seconds sixty people were rushing down the hallway towards the hole in the floor where the Stargrazer was docked.

"Move it!" yelled Eddie as he fired blaster beams into the now smoke filled hallway before him. On the opposite side of the hallway from him, ducking behind a protrusion in the wall Red waited for his hand cannon to recharge. An instant later he stepped from behind the protection and braced his legs as the cannon fired a massive pulse of energy through the air towards the gathered guards. The deafeningly loud 'Whoomp!' sound it roared made the freed captives cover their ears while some squealed in surprise as they dropped through into the Stargrazer.

"Things're gonna be tight in there, so get as far back as you can," Eddie shouted.

Reynolds, the female scientist who had spoken to Dan a moment earlier grabbed his shoulder as she was running past, ducking down behind him. "Where's the boss?"

"On the Cag, runnin' interference, now get on board hon, we ain't got time ta waste."

She nodded and dropped through the hole between the Stargrazer and the station. Instantly the artificial gravity in the Stargrazer took hold of her as the instant she stepped through the hole she was suddenly standing on what a second ago within the station would have been the ceiling, but aboard the 'Grazer was actually its floor, which was attached to the floor of the station. In other words when she stepped into the 'Grazer, everything as upside down.

Again the former captives heard the explosion of Red's gun as Eddie continued to fire into the smoke filled miasma ahead of him. Energy blasts were being fired in answer now back upon the Stargrazer's crew from within the smoke.

"All clear down here!" Dan shouted.

"Everyone's aboard." Eddie replied.

"Let's move it!" Red shouted.

Dan came thundering down the hallway, his feet pounding upon the floor like heavy drums, as behind him from the opposite end of the hallway energy blasts began to smack his armored form and the walls of the hallway about him.

Eddie dropped through the hole into the Stargrazer followed by Red. Dan suddenly stopped behind them as blaster beams seared his armor all about him.

He stood there watching impassively as enemies moved closer and closer to him, now no longer hidden in the fog-like smoke. Within his helmet he grinned as he jammed both his hands into the wall on his right and tore the entire wall down for thirty feet in both directions, burying the enemy combatants. "That's what ya get for killin' our friends, and taking the rest captive." He turned his head towards a camera he had seen earlier, mounted on the ceiling above him, and then growled menacingly, "Don't mess with us." Then he leaped up, and crushed the camera in one massive paw.

An instant later he dropped through the hole in the floor just before the Stargrazer's belly hatch irised closed. People were jammed like sardines in the small ship, but he fought his way to the front, even as Eddie ramped the engines up to full power and the Stargrazer hurtled away from the station as the stations defenses came to life, firing blasts at the diminutive ship, coloring space like a lightning storm at night.

Dan moved into his seat, taking flight control from Eddie.

"Well that was certainly exciting." A baldheaded man said, elbowing his way up to the front of the ship to stand behind Dan's seat.

"Hang on tight Moratora." Dan looked over his shoulder at the man.

"I am. As tightly as possible, Mr. Sledge."

"Good, 'cause we ain't outta the woods yet."

Even as Dan spoke, the small ship was rocked by explosions as energy blasts seared its shields.

"Red, what's goin' on?" Dan asked, plunging the ship hard astern. Behind them, the crew heard gasps and cries of surprise as the former captives were thrown about.

"What do you think is going on? They're shooting at us!"

"I kinda figured that one out, genius."

"Dan, get us to hyper-warp, man. We can't out fight those things," Eddie shouted.

"What things?" The beleaguered pilot replied.

Red punched a button on his control panel and the view screen split in half, showing both fore and aft views side by side. In the aft one, a huge war ship was speeding after them, and gaining rapidly.

Dan looked in surprise and then grimaced, "I thought they were all taken out by the Cag?"

"Well obviously not all of them," Red answered sarcastically.

Dan shook his head angrily, "Everybody hang onto somethin'. This is gonna get rough."

He touched a control and the ship leaped into hyper-warp, leaving their pursuers far behind.

"Full power to the engines, divert extra power to the rear shields. We took a beating already. We can't take a chance on getting' hit again."

"Where to now?" the bald man named Moratora asked.

"We rendezvous with the Cag. That's step number one. After that we have to get back to Earth, and warn everyone."

"What are you talking about? You can't warn anyone in time to save the planet? These people have hundreds maybe thousands of ships that can break the light barrier. Counting this one, Earth has two." The auburn haired woman, Reynolds said, coming up to stand next to Moratora.

"It ain't a matter a goin' faster than light once we get back there; it's gonna be a matter of 'who's got the bigger guns?' So far from everything I've seen, that's definitely us, lady"

"Dan's right, Reynolds," Red began, "Earth has hundreds of ships between the planet and Pluto. All armed to the teeth. From what I've seen, in my professional opinion since we've been out here, they haven't got a chance against us."

Reynolds snorted and threw her mane of auburn hair back as she laughed. "You jokers make me laugh. Do you really think these aliens can't handle backwards ol' us? We're the new kids in town, and these guys will smack us down like nothing."

"Really Reynolds? And why'd you think of something like that?"

"Because how else could it end? If this alien race has been keeping its eyes on Earth and our developments, then why shouldn't they be ready for any weapon we've got? My God, they impersonated the General and put a plant right in the pentagon while doing so. We're up against some serious bad guys. This is not going to be a joke or an easy mission."

"No kiddin' lady," Dan rumbled, "Though it don't much matter. This is somethin' we have to do. If we don't warn home in time, our families will be massacred by these aliens, as well as everyone else on the planet."

"They're an advanced race, or races, if they wanted to pluck us out of the stars they could do so with ease," Reynolds replied hotly.

Red turned to her, with anger flashing across his face, "Lady, are you kidding me? We have won at every turn here."

"Except the one where forty of us were slaughtered and the other sixty were captured while you fools were off playing space cowboys," she retorted with equal ire.

"Do you think the boss or any of us aren't going to feel that one for a long time, sister? You had better think again. Now go claim a spot away from me, before I throw cuffs on your wrists and a rag in your mouth. I'm still head of security on this ship. You don't want to piss me off."

Her eyes bulged from her face as she glared at him then she slowly turned and walked away, disappearing into the back of the crowded ship.

"What got into her?" Eddie asked.

"She's afraid," Red replied. "Very afraid. I'd say the vast majority of these people never expected what happened to them to happen in the first place. It was never even a consideration."

Eddie nodded, "Yeah I get that. But hey, they were all warned before we took off. But besides that, I think we better keep an eye on Reynolds. Something ain't right. I mean how'd she know all that stuff about the General? She wasn't there and was already taken captive by the time we got back."

"Good point Eddie." Red replied, "She's got my attention now."

Eddie nodded, "It's still terrible about our people though. But everyone did know the consequences and came along on their own. There's just nothing we can do about it now.

"Maybe so Eddie, but how long are we gonna be able ta hide behind that one?" Dan asked quietly, "This is tearin' the boss up, just like the rest of us."

"Right now we have to look at the big picture, and that's getting back to Earth and warning everyone." Red interrupted.

"You're right, Red. How far to the rendezvous coordinates?"

"Another hour at one hundred percent throttle in hyper-warp."

"Not that bad." Danny replied. "Any activity behind us?"

"Not yet, but you know they'll be coming."

"I know. Even if the Cag did manage to cripple a few of them, that automated firing pass Mark did had to leave a few ships able to break through the FTL barrier."

"That's what I'm worried about, Dan."

"Yeah, me too, Red."

Eddie turned and looked back at the people standing behind him in the crowded ship before finally speaking, "Everyone all right back there? Anybody hurt?"

There were few murmurings but finally a young woman pushed her way to the front and began speaking, "There are several hurt back here, boys, but nothing serious. A few broken bones and some scrapes and bruises." As she spoke she touched her own face, which sported a black and blue bruise on her cheek without thinking. She was a pretty young woman, with long black hair and a slender body. Her face was almost pixie-ish with rosy cheeks despite what she had been through. She stood a mere five feet tall.

Dan turned towards her and smiled gently, "Thanks Dr. Troiano. We'll have you back in your medical bay in no time. You and your staff will be able to get to work helping these people as soon as possible."

She returned his smile, with a hint of weariness in her eyes. "We're already on it Dan. Things are cramped back here, but we're doing what we can. Just get us to the ship as soon as you can, please. A lot of people are uncomfortable."

Dan nodded, "Understood Doc."

Eddie looked to his two friends, and then with a sigh asked the one thing none of them wanted to think about, "I wonder how Mark and Ariel are doing?"

Chapter Fifteen

"They have us surrounded!" Ariel shouted, as Mark heaved the Cagliostro to starboard.

"I know Ari, I can see," he answered hotly.

The Cagliostro corkscrewed through space, avoiding energy beams from three war ships that each dwarfed it.

"This is not getting to be any more fun the longer we're doing it," Ariel again snorted.

"Ari! Enough!" Mark barked at her, as he heaved the ship to port feverishly. He was watching sensor readouts before him, and based on computer projections, trying to avoid enemy fire. At times he was successful. More times he wasn't.

The great ships shields and energy levels were holding this time though, and not being drained.

Mark tapped a panel on his virtual control screen and began to talk, "General, how're you doing down there?"

"So far so good, Johnson. Just get us to the rendezvous point."

"That's just what I'm trying to do General." Mark hit the comm button again and closed the conversation.

If one were to watch the battle unfolding on the outside of the Cagliostro's hull it would seem like a video game, as the great manta ray shaped ship spun and looped then returned fire with pin point accuracy, leaving jagged scars across their hulls.

"I don't get this," Ariel began, "How are we doing more damage to them than they are to us?"

"Don't kid yourself Ari, any other ship from Earth would be very damaged right now. When I said our hull and shields were state of the art, I wasn't kidding around. This is one tough ship. As far as us doing damage to them, we're Earthmen, we know how to break things," he replied with a half grin.

"No kidding, ace."

Again the Cag rocked as several blasts raked its hull. Again the lighting dimmed and then immediately returned to full brightness.

"Hang on tight Ari, things are about to get rough."

"About to?" She asked, wide-eyed.

The ship spun and dove below one of the war ships that was approaching them. These ships were akin to mile long blocks of granite. They had no real shape to them, no sleekness. Just weapons and nothing more. They were not made for fast maneuvers, only attacking. Mark dove the Cagliostro in close to the huge enemy ship's hull, fairly skimming against it.

Once there, he trained all the Cags weapons directly ahead of them and fired, slashing a groove into the war ships length. As the Cag darted away, he let two missiles fly free, they turned about in space and arced directly back to the ship they had just attacked. The missiles exploded within the deep grooves the Cag's solar cannons had just cut. An instant later the ship itself exploded into atoms. As it did, Mark hit hyper-warp and the Cagliostro disappeared in an eruption of light.

"Well I'm sure that did it, if nothing else before had." Ariel commented.

"Did what?" Mark replied.

"Declared war on an alien civilization."

"Sorry honey, they did that to us when they set up a hidden base on our world, kidnapped a very high ranking General and replaced him with a clone under their control, whoever 'they' are."

She sighed, exasperated, "Mark, I'm not arguing that point with you, believe me. I know they attacked us first, and we had no choice but to respond. Hell they tortured and killed almost half of our crew—the crew of a peaceful, non-military vessel."

"Exactly Ariel. Our only course was to respond in kind, in at least trying to meet them surreptitiously and finding out the most we could. We both saw how all that worked out with the aforementioned crew."

"Well, you just blew up one of their ships, and damaged almost forty more. That should piss them off to no end," she replied.

"No kidding. It should also let them know we are deadly serious and won't be afraid to respond in kind to whatever they try to throw at us."

"Again," she answered, "whoever 'they' are."

"Yes, that goes without saying. But I'm willing to bet they know who we are now."

"You're right, but that doesn't mean it's a good thing."

"No, you're right." A small signal light blinked on his control panel as it began to beep at the same time.

"What's that?" Ariel asks.

"The rendezvous coordinates. I'm slowing to full stop, but keeping shields raised."

Ariel nodded in agreement as the ship dropped out of hyper-warp and slowed to a stop.

"Now we wait for the Stargrazer to catch up." Mark stated flatly.

"Do you think they're okay?" She asked, concern written all over her beautiful face.

"Yes, they have to be. Everything is riding on them being 'okay'."

As if in answer to his thoughts, the Stargrazer dropped out of hyper-warp practically on top of the Cagliostro.

"I've got Dan on the comm," Ariel offered.

"Put him on."

The view screen lit up with Dan Sledge's face. "Man, am I happy to see you two. Permission to come aboard?" Behind Dan could be seen a great mass of people stuffed tightly together within the confines of the small ship.

"Gladly Mr. Sledge, welcome home. Make it fast though, I've no doubt that we'll have company and soon. After what we just did, it's not going to be a happy group coming to invite us over for tea and crumpets, that's for certain."

"Okay boss, tell me all about it when we get settled in."

"Will do Danny, opening the landing bay doors now. As soon as you're in, we're out of here."

As Mark was talking, the Stargrazer was already coming to a rest within the Cagliostro. The little sixty foot long ship gently touched down as the landing bay doors closed behind it.

Sledge exited the Stargrazer and found Abruzzi standing there next to the powered up and running fleet of shuttles. All three of them had their magno-disc engines running. "How'd this work out?" Dan asked, as he walked over several heavy, thick cables lying on the floor and linking the shuttles to the Cagliostro.

"It did the trick, son. It's how Johnson overcame the lettuce-heads power siphoning beam." As they were speaking, the Cagliostro suddenly powered up and leapt into hyper-warp. They could feel the transition within the landing bay.

"He ran the shuttles?"

"Yes he did, son, and it was a damned brilliant plan too. He said something about shield frequencies and power outputs backing up this ships with the shuttles. Some nonsensical gobbledy gook like that."

"What he did, that was pretty ingenious, General." Dan shook his head as he began to walk out of the landing bay. Behind him all sixty people were out and the ones who were unhurt or with minor injuries were hurrying back to their posts. The more severely injured were lying down in the landing bay, awaiting Dr.Trioano's and her staff's ministrations.

She shooed him out of the landing bay as Red and Eddie joined him in running down the corridor and entering a maglovator. "I hope they didn't waste too much time there waiting fer us." Sledge began.

"Even if they did, it had to happen." Eddie replied

"Yeah that's right, Dan. But we're back now. Let's get to the command deck and compare notes there." Red answered.

"Sounds good to me." They exited the maglovator on to the command deck, and a moment later the General did likewise behind them.

Everyone gathered, and began to speak.

"Well, we're all up to date and on the same page at least." Mark affirmed.

"Lotta good that's gonna do us if we can't get them back home to believe us."

"That's going to be up to the General, Danny."

"Me?" Abruzzi reacted in shock.

"Yes sir, you. You have to convince them the man posing as you is an imposter, and that you are the real McCoy."

"That's going to be easier said than done."

"It doesn't matter, General. It has to be done, or everyone on our world is lost to us. I have no doubt those aliens are not too far behind us. I think we're faster than they are, but that doesn't mean anything if no one back home acknowledges this threat as real."

"How far away are we from sub-space range?" Abruzzi asked.

"Ariel's been broadcasting for the past hour, a recorded loop, when we get a reply, we'll go live. But to be honest I'm figuring that it'll be days before they receive our message."

Abruzzi puffed out his chest, then exhaled before speaking, "Well, what kind of message did you leave them?"

"That we have information vital to Earth's continued survival, and that I don't want to give any more than that away until we're face to face."

"Well, it don't matter," Dan began, "We're so far off it'll take us three days at one hundred percent power just to arrive at the outer reaches of our galaxy."

"Don't worry Dan, the Cag can take it. She's a tough bird." Ariel affirmed, smiling.

"Believe me, Ariel, I know that better than anybody. Don't forget, Mark and I designed most of the systems on this baby from his ideas."

"What if they don't believe us?" the General asked.

"It won't matter General, I have one other trump card to play yet."

"What is it?" Abruzzi asked, intrigued.

"In due time General, in due time. For now let's just concentrate on getting out of this galaxy and evading any ships that may be hiding in wait for us between here and Earth."

The General 'harrumphed' once, then sat in the same seat he had occupied earlier. "The sooner we get home the better. This whole damned mess has left me itching to see Earth again. It's been too long. Some of you may have been made for all this otherworldly adventure, but the rest of us are definitely not."

Mark smiled before replying, "Duly noted, General, and thank you for all your help, by the way."

"I have to help, son. I'm not turning my back on planet and country now. Both need this old man. Plus, I need some payback on those salad heads for keeping me captive all that time."

"How long did they have you?" Ariel asked.

"I don't even know for certain, Ariel."

"When was the last time we met and talked before they took you?" Mark asked.

"You had just started construction on this ship. The frame wasn't in place yet."

"That's impossible." Mark answered, obviously surprised.

"Why?" the old man replied.

"Because General, that was three years ago."

Chapter Sixteen

"Return weapons fire!" Mark shouted as the Cagliostro rocked once again.

Three days had passed since they had escaped their pursuers from the space station. It had been a three days filled with fleeting attacks from various alien ships

On the view screen the ship attacking them was different this time. It was sleek and smaller than the huge war ships that had dogged their trail the past three days. This one was almost avian shaped, akin to a hunting hawk diving towards prey. It maneuvered as well as the Cagliostro did, that much was already evident. Both ships danced through space, returning fire on each other again and again.

"Direct hit, Mark." Eddie shouted, "I scored them good with that one."

"Less talk, more firing, Eddie. Destroy that ship."

Eddie shot Mark an annoyed glance over his shoulder as Dan rolled the Cag over and over through space. But the hawk ship mimicked the Cagliostro's move perfectly.

"This is gettin' ridiculous." Dan complained.

"I thought you were good at what you did?" Eddie verbally jabbed Dan.

"Yeah, big mouth? When you actually hit somethin' then open yer yap. So far you're what? One for forty?"

"At least I did hit something. This guy is matching you move for move, and it looks like he's doing it pretty easily too."

"Both of you shut up." Mark ordered, "Dan, go back to hyper warp, full power to the engines. Let them chase us. Double rear shields. Now you're going to see why I designed three solar cannons at the rear of the ship."

"Everybody hang on," Dan roared as he flipped the ship over and accelerated directly at and then above and past the ship that was following them, passing cleanly above the enemy vessel, then immediately disappearing into hyper-warp.

"That ship will be on our tail any second." Red stated.

"No kidding, Sherlock." Dan answered.

"Will both of you stop arguing and listen? Red, you let me know when that ship appears on the rear sensors. Eddie switch your view to rear also. When that thing shows, drop our speed down to ninety-eight percent. Let it catch up, slowly."

"You want it to catch us?" Ariel asked.

"I want it to get closer to us, not catch us. That ship seems to be a match for the Cag in every way. Beyond the body design, I'm willing to bet it's a copy of the Cag."

"What? How?"

"They replaced the General, who else could they have replaced? Someone in the company as well, I'm willing to bet, someone close to the designs. It could have been anyone. I'll have to come up with a way to distinguish a clone from the original and scan everyone back at the company when we get this straightened out."

"Why would they copy our ship? We're the new guys. This makes no sense." Eddie almost shouted.

"It makes perfect sense, Eddie. All these races have been watching Earth for a reason. It's what I said earlier, they fear us. We make good stuff."

"That doesn't even sound like proper English." Ariel chuckled drily.

"It probably isn't, but that's not what I'm concerned about right now. Have they caught up yet, Red?"

"Just coming into sensor range now."

"Excellent. Can you get a reading on their shields?"

"They are fully deployed, and at full power."

"Good, now how do they compare to ours?"

"What?"

"Our shields Red, how do they compare to our shields?"

"Uhhh, they look solid. Very solid."

"Read their frequency. Are they the same as ours? Chances are they are exactly the same. Fighting this ship has been like fighting our own ship, in every way."

Suddenly the Cagliostro rocked as several energy blasts slammed into the ships rear shields.

"And there they are, right on schedule as expected."

Mark sat back in his seat and brought up a virtual control panel. "Here we go." The ship rocked again as blasts again impacted on their shields.

"Mark, what are you doing?" Dan asked quietly.

Mark raised his hand toward Dan for silence, "Eddie I'm sending a command to your firing control panel. When you fire, that signal is going to ride along with the canons pulse."

"Mark, what the hell are you talking about?" Eddie asked, without removing his eyes from the firing panel.

"Eddie, just fire, will you? Center cannon only on first volley, please. Red, bring up the aft of the ship on the main view screen please."

The view screen switched to the rear of the ship as the center cannon fired a blast that hit the pursuing ship's shields, suddenly illuminating them in a pattern of squares across the front of the enemy ship. The squares glowed brightly in a flash and then went out.

"NOW!" shouted Mark while enthusiastically pumping his fist, "Full power all rear cannons."

The three rear mounted solar cannons blasted streams of glowing energy from their tips, slamming through the shields as if they were non-existent and exploding upon the ship's hull, cascading across its surface, and spinning the pursuer sideways off course with their power.

"Eddie, again!" Mark roared. Eddie nodded and stabbed the fire control again, repeatedly. All three cannons fired multiple times, each hit and spun the pursuer violently twice more, until the ship suddenly exploded into its component atoms, lighting up the view screen like an exploding star.

"What the hell?" Red exclaimed.

"A failsafe. He built a failsafe into the shield codes." Dan chuckled lowly.

"You shut off their shields. That's—that's cheating." Ariel stumbled upon her own words in surprise, an astonished look creeping over her face.

"No, cloning and replacing people, and seeking to undermine my company and our planet, *that's* cheating, and so much more."

"So now what?" Eddie asked, bemused at what just happened.

"We get to Earth, as quickly as possible." Mark replied grimly.

"We're approaching the outskirts of the solar system now, Mark."

"Okay Danny, thanks."

"Uhhh, Mark, you better look at this." Red suddenly exclaimed. He adjusted a control on his virtual control panel and the view screen suddenly zoomed in on a point in space several million miles ahead of them.

"Uh oh," Eddie almost whispered.

"That ain't good." Dan added.

"Mark?" Ariel turned toward him, her face blank with fear.

For his part Mark Johnson said nothing, He just stared at the view screen and shook his head grimly.

Before them in a far reaching ring of ships was a blockade spread out as far as the eye could see.

Dan turned towards him, "Mark, those ain't the alien ships."

"I know Dan, those are all Earth fleet vessels."

"Maybe they got the messages we've been broadcasting and are here to help us, in case we were being followed," Eddie offered.

"I don't think so," Ariel began as she turned towards Mark, a worried look upon her face, "I just received a message ordering us to surrender, from General Abruzzi, and the President."

Chapter Seventeen

General Abruzzi, the *real* General Abruzzi stood up from his seat behind Mark's chair and stared angrily at the view screen. "That's every ship in the fleet. They have hundreds of them out there all to capture us? That's not making any sense. They left Earth totally unprotected."

"Yes General, it does make sense. Perfect sense actually."

"How, Johnson?"

"They're out here looking for us, which leaves Earth unprotected."

"I wouldn't say it was unprotected, son. There are plenty of land based, and satellite defenses in play. Those alone should be able to defend the planet against just about any attack."

"That we know of, General. There are something like two hundred fifty ships from the United States alone here, never mind every other nation on the planet. What if thousands of ships descend on Earth from all over the galaxy? Then what?"

"Well if there are thousands of ships coming we're not going to have much of a chance anyway, Johnson."

"Something's not right. Dan, come to full stop."

"Okay, boss." Sledge replied.

"Mark, what are you thinking?" Ariel asked.

"Ari, if they have thousands of ships, why haven't they just attacked us already? Long ago? The United States has about two hundred and fifty ships at this point, all war ships capable of leveling cities from space. No nation has close to that. China has half that number. Russia bankrupted itself trying to keep up. It's what led to the fall of their new progressive party. England has what? A hundred ships at best? So let's say that in total earth has about five hundred spaceships, not starships, but spaceships, because right now, this is the only starship from Earth. This is the only ship, not counting the Stargrazer, which can break the light speed barrier and attain full hyper-warp flight through space."

Abruzzi looked at Mark quizzically, "I'm not following where you're going with this, son."

"There's a big question hanging over our heads here General and it's a simple one. Why? Why go through all of this? Why the kidnappings, the cloning's, why build a base under the Blue Ridge mountains for God's sake?"

"Control?" asked Ariel.

"Yes, but control of what? Our government? Our world? Our space program?"

"Well they lost any shot at that once it became privatized and guys like you came along." Dan replied.

"That's somewhat true Dan, and maybe a good reason for this, as in they, whoever 'they' are, had to take a firmer hand in our supposed self-destruction."

"Ya know, you're not even mentionin' the eight hundred pound monkey in the room." Dan said.

"I know, I haven't gotten to that yet, but we might as well broach the subject now. They have the President. There is no feasible way the real President would stand with the imposter Abruzzi, especially since he sent us on this mission."

"What if he was the imposter all along?" Red offered.

"What do you mean Red?"

"Mark, think about it, he sends us off across space, looking for the General," Red pointed at the General sitting in a seat on the walkway behind them, "figuring we'd either all be killed, captured or the Cag would be destroyed by the superior alien tech."

"So you think this faux President sent us on a wild goose chase, hopefully to our doom."

"That would make sense exceptin' for one thing," Dan interjected as he jerked his thumb behind him, "We got the real Abruzzi sittin' here behind us."

"Yes, that is an excellent point, Dan." Mark agreed, "But not out of the question in regards to Red's scenario." He stood up now and began pacing back and forth around the command deck. "Let's say the real President sent us on this mission. Let's say he wasn't taken hostage until after we left and he was replaced with another clone. So now we have to locate the real President."

"But we already know where they would hold him prisoner." Ariel smiled.

"Of course we do," Mark answered, smiling broadly, "Below the Blue Ridge mountain section nearest to Washington."

"Right where we found the General." Red smiled broadly, "But then it was on the copy of the Blue Ridge on another world.

"Exactly." Mark replied. "Now all we have to do is get there, and free him."

"You know this is not going to be as easy as it was to free the General?" Red grinned.

"I don't remember that bein' easy at all." Dan replied with a smirk.

"Never mind that, how far are we from the blockade, or rather where is it in relation to Earth?" Mark asked.

"It's between Mars and Jupiter. They're using the asteroid belt itself to take up space, and sort of clog the path home." Red answered.

"Good plan." Abruzzi approved, "Someone knows tactics."

"We have to assume they have our own people planning this entire blockade out." Mark thought aloud, while still pacing.

"Why not? For all they know they're helping stop the dangerous Mark Johnson and his crew of traitors." Red suggested.

"Very true. So we have to now assume we are wanted, accused traitors and public enemy's number one through five."

"But again, we have the General to disprove their claims."

"Unless they claim he is the clone and not the man with them." Eddie replied.

Mark threw his hands upward, then sat down once again before continuing, "We could go back and forth about this for the next week and get nowhere. Bottom line-we have to get to Virginia, free the President from that underground bunker and take back control of the nation. If we don't, well I don't think whatever they have planned out for us all will be all that pleasant, and by 'us all' I mean everyone on Earth."

"Okay boss, where do we start?" Dan Sledge asked.

Mark walked over behind him and placed his hand on Dan's shoulder, "Tell me Danny, have you ever run a blockade before?"

Chapter Eighteen

"This ain't gonna be fun." Dan grumbled, as the Cagliostro powered up and streaked away towards Earth.

"Prepare to go to hyper-warp, Mr. Sledge." Mark commanded.

"Oh I'm ready an' waitin' for this one, boss man, just say when."

"I think now would be good." Mark replied as the ship suddenly streaked away at faster than light speed, heading directly towards the asteroid belt and the blockade of war ships, each five times the size of the Cagliostro.

"How long until we appear on their scanners, Red?"

"About another ten seconds, Mark."

"Okay, double front shields, Red. We could get a little singed on this one, people."

"You have a way with words you know." Ariel smirked.

"So you've told me on more than one occasion," he replied with a wink.

"Brace yourselves, here it comes!" grunted Red, as the ship was rocked by energy beam fire that raked across the front shields, mercilessly. The ship vibrated and shook with each hit, as crew members all over the great vessel grit their teeth and prayed.

"Red, how long until we're past them?"

"Another thirty seconds, Mark, and once we get past them they'll never catch us. It'll take them two weeks to get back to Earth."

The Cagliostro soared at hyper-warp speed, hurtling through space, spinning and flipping, as Dan worked hard to avoid their getting hit by the powerful war ships energy blasts. Sometimes he was successful, sometimes not.

"Hey, Dan," Eddie called, "How about trying not to get us hit by every blast, okay? Maybe try to miss just a few?" Eddie grinned nervously.

"I should throw you out a hatch right now, short stuff," Dan grumbled as he fought the controls.

"Stow it you two, let's just get through this," Mark ordered, "Red, report?"

"Shields at forty eight percent and dropping, boss. That's a lot of firepower out there and all of it aimed at us."

"I know, Red. Begin to rotate shield power to the rear of the ship immediately upon completing our pass."

The Cagliostro flew past the blockade, flying on edge as it streaked between two mammoth war ships, each firing continually at the much smaller manta ray shaped ship. Each scoring several glancing blasts off the brightly glowing rear shields.

"How are they even seeing us? We're traveling so fast, we should be almost invisible," Ariel asked.

"They don't see us. It's the long range tracking and aiming systems that I sold to the military two years ago. They begin to track movements from half a star system away, and do a damned good job of firing on a target with an almost clairvoyant aim."

"In other words you build good stuff."

"Yes, and for once that actually goes against us, though like I do with everything I build, I built in a failsafe." Mark paused a second, then turned towards Red, "Red what is our shield strength right now?"

Red smiled nervously before answering, "Four percent."

"Talk about a close call..." Eddie murmured.

"You know Johnson," Abruzzi interrupted, "If you have little secrets that the government shouldn't know about, you shouldn't be bringing them out in the open when one of the leaders of the military is sitting behind you."

"Doesn't much matter, sir," Mark turned to face him, smirking, "You're as much of a fugitive right now as we are."

"Yes. I know Johnson, but if we get through this all, we may end up on opposite sides of something some time from now. I'm a loyal American, son, always bear that in mind when speaking around me."

"General, we all are, everyone here I mean," the crew looked at Abruzzi and nodded seriously.

"Glad to hear it son, I didn't have any doubts either, just in case you were wondering." The big, white haired, old man shifted in his seat, his mustache moving upon his upper lip as he inhaled hard.

"No issue here, General, just sit back and enjoy the show."

Mark called up a virtual control panel and began adjusting controls as the Cagliostro streaked towards Earth. They were well beyond the blockade now. Mark hit a few last buttons and adjusted a virtual dial.

"We're coming into weapons range of the satellite net now Mark." Red pronounced.

"All right Red, thank you. We should be good to go at this point. Stay your course Mr. Sledge, the one I just programmed in. Make sure we drop out of hyper-warp before we hit the atmosphere. Too long an exposure will burn us up like paper in fire."

"Dropping out now Chief," Dan replied.

The Cagliostro slowed gracefully, though if one were looking at the view screen it seemed the Earth suddenly appeared on the monitor, seemingly from nowhere. Everyone on the command deck, except for Mark, inhaled sharply at the sight of the Earth suddenly just appearing there.

Mark simply smiled.

Dan adjusted his controls, eased the ship past the satellites in orbit and down towards the Earth. Once past, Mark again punched in commands on his control panel and then shut it down. The virtual control panel faded from view as if it was never there.

"What just happened?" Eddie asked.

"I shut down their sensor arrays. Then, once we were past them, I turned them back on," Mark smiled.

"So you have the codes to shut down our entire defensive network? I don't like that one bit, Johnson," the General grunted.

"General, it was a one time, one use fail safe. I can't do it again. Now that I turned them all back on, their codes shuffled and I have no idea what they are."

Abruzzi leaned back in his seat once more, scowling.

"Mark, the coordinates that you punched in here are taking us directly to the Blue Ridge mountain range. It's going to be a little tough to hide a thousand foot long starship there, or even to find a landing spot," Red began.

"Yes Mr. Robinski, I am aware of that."

"You may be aware of that, but what are you going to do about it?" Red retorted.

"Working on it Red, relax a moment." Mark stood from his seat, took a step forward and knelt lower above Dan's control panel next to the big man.

"Right there," he pointed at a spot on Sledge's control panel. Dan nodded as the ship slowed and descended towards it all but silently.

An instant later the Cagliostro touched to the ground, seemingly as light as a feather.

"Activating reflective skin," Red announced.

"Reflective what?" the General asked, obviously annoyed.

Mark turned toward him and replied lightly, it's experimental, General. It is something I haven't perfected yet."

"Well it sounds like it could mean invisibility on the battlefield or something like it."

" 'Something like it' is a better approximation, at least right now. It reflects our surroundings back upon the ships hide. It works better at night but not at all in space, where I was hoping it would work. I have to perfect it yet, so that's why as of now it is not for sale. Once it's perfected, you'll hear about it, General."

Abruzzi nodded.

"So what now Mark?" Red asked.

"Now we raid an enemy base, and seek to save the President, who should be buried and hidden here underground."

"I don't think you should use the word 'buried' right now, Mark," Eddie smirked.

"Yeah you are right Eddie, but let's get our acts together people, on the ground in three minutes." He tapped a button on his just re-appeared virtual control panel and spoke into a microphone that appeared there. "Secondary command crew to the command deck."

The primary command crew stood and flexed stiff muscles, exiting the deck as the secondary crew took their places. Mark looked on as a young man entered the command deck, smiled somewhat nervously, nodded to him and then took the Captain's chair. His mind drifted back to his young protégé and friend, the murdered Miles Jefferson in remorse. Now this young man sat in the command chair nodding stoically at Mark. Mark vowed silently that the same fate would not befall this brave young man.

"Mr. Marek, good to see you up and about," Mark chided, "Take care of my bird while I'm gone, and do not, I repeat, do not get a scratch on her gleaming hide, am I clear?"

He finished with a smile.

Marek smiled cautiously, not knowing if Mark was joking with him or not, and nodded, "Nothing to worry about sir. I'll guard her with my life."

"Don't do anything stupid. Seriously, Matt." Johnson replied. "If you see any trouble get her out of here, and up into space, as fast as possible."

"What about y'all?" Matt Marek asked with a slight southern drawl.

"Don't worry about us. The ship is the important thing."

"Whatever you say, boss." The young man replied nervously.

Mark headed towards the maglovator before turning back to the man who sat in the command chair, "Don't sweat it, kid, you'll do fine."

Marek nodded, and then Mark stepped into the maglovator and was gone.

***

The crew exited the great ship, which sat in a clearing. The reflective skin mirrored the ship's surroundings and the ship seemed to be effectively hidden. Mark, Ariel, Red, Dan and Eddie began silently walking up an incline. Ariel had already mentally linked them all upon exiting the ship.

'*Does this look familiar?*' Mark asked through the link.

'*Yeah it does,*' replied Red, '*They terraformed that area to look like this back on that desert world.*'

He was, at that point, trudging up the mountain, followed by Dan and Eddie. All were armed, with Red carrying his preferred weapon, the hand held cannon he had used on the space station. Dan carried two energy pistols, and Eddie held an energy rifle as he scanned ahead of them and to the sides. Mark walked in the back of the pack with Ariel.

'*Are you 'hearing' anything yet?*' Mark asked Ari as they made their way upwards.

'*Just our thoughts, no one else's,*' she replied.

'Well if this plays to form, we should be near enough to our entrance any second now. Anyone see, hear or even smell anything?'

'There has to be guards out here,' Red broadcasted mentally.

'I know, it don't make sense that there isn't,' Dan replied.

Mark's hand scanner was still reading all clear.

"You are all under arrest," a familiar amplified voice boomed out around them, "Stay where you are, and you will not be harmed."

'Ari,' Mark warned through the psychic link, *'tell the Cag to get out of here.'*

'Already done, I screamed it in Marek's mind the instant that voice boomed out.'

Behind them, a flash of light disappearing into the sky was the only remnant of the Cagliostro's silent departure.

'Now we're really on our own,' Eddie mentally murmured.

"You five will come with me." A voice intruded on their thoughts. They turned toward the sound of that voice as it exited a camouflaged bunker door, with a dozen troops, all with weapons drawn.

Dan was the first to react, "It's that guy again, the purple skinned lettuce head from that desert planet."

"No, it's not," Mark corrected, "It's another just like him."

"Very astute, Mr. Johnson. My 'brother' as it were is one of many of us who are in command of these facilities across the galaxy.

The uniformed alien stood facing them, with his hands behind his back, as he continued to speak.

But Ariel wasn't looking at this man. She was staring at the creature behind him. The Quel met her gaze unemotionally. She locked her eyes with those of the mental parasite, and stared unwaveringly at him.

"You will all come with me now. Your interrogations will begin immediately." The purple skinned alien announced as they were led through the doorway into the concrete bunker and down steps made of the same material.

He turned towards Mark and pointed, "We will begin with you."

Chapter Nineteen

Mark Johnson knelt on the ground, his hands tied behind his back, and spat blood out of his mouth. As he did, the big alien before him punched him across the jaw once again, knocking him back to the cold, hard, cement floor. He grunted as two more lettuce heads—as the rest of his crew called them—reached over and pushed him back to a kneeling position. Mark spit blood directly at his tormentor this time, as the big salad head reared back for another punch.

"Enough." A voice called out, and slowly the owner of that voice, the purple skinned lettuce headed alien that had been in command of the group that had grabbed them outside this underground compound walked into the light from behind the tormentor. "This will go so much easier on you, Mr. Johnson, if you simply tell us what we want to know. Where are your worlds ship emplacements in space, what is the code that shuts down the defense satellite network, and finally, where is your ship?"

Mark spat blood once again, and then smiled. "Let's be perfectly clear about this 'Radicchio head', if I knew any of those things, which I really do not, I wouldn't tell you. You can kill me, you'll never get anything out of me, because A) I really don't know anything you're asking me, and B) as far as I'm concerned you can really go screw off. I'm never going to be a traitor to not only my nation but my world as well. Kill me now. Nothing is ever going to change my answer."

The alien, instead of looking angry or non-plussed merely shrugged his shoulders and spoke simply, "We shall see."

He turned back and walked outside the cell area. "Bring the girl."

Mark knew this was coming, it was only a matter of time. Two more salad heads dragged Ariel in. Her beautiful face was bruised and blood dripped from her mouth as well. Her sleeves and uniform top were torn.

Mark stood up, despite the bonds on his hands and feet, "You bastards." He grunted as she fell towards him, barely conscious. He moved under her, catching her weight between his neck and his shoulder, then slowly he collapsed to the ground, easing her down.

"We shall leave you both alone for a while. You see Mr. Johnson, my dinner is being served, and I do not want it to be cold." The salad head in charge commented as he walked out of the cell, the three interrogators followed him with the laser grid activating behind them as they walked out silently and disappeared down the hallway.

Mark cradled Ariel's head on his shoulder as she moaned quietly.

"This is another fine mess you've gotten me into, Johnson," she smiled as best she could.

"Stop it," he chastised. "You're hurt, badly enough that I'm very worried right now.

"Iss only a scratch." She hissed through bloody teeth, matching his own, as her eyes closed and she mercilessly, quietly passed out.

'*We're in trouble.*' Mark thought to himself. '*But I refuse to give in, or surrender. We'll get out of this one, the only question is how?*'

***

Ninety three million miles away—give or take a few— the Cagliostro hid behind the Sun. Using the giant stars radiations to mask its presence from the war ships that now hurtled towards Earth in search of the star cruiser and its crew. Matt Marek sat nervously in the command chair, as several officers awaited his commands.

"Any of you have any type of suggestion that might save them without us getting our heads blown off?" Marek asked.

"I have one," a new voice intruded as its owner entered the command deck from the maglovator. Marek turned and saw Reynolds standing there, the auburn haired scientist who had argued with Eddie and Red aboard the Stargrazer. "Surrender."

"Are you nuts lady?" Marek replied, his voice one step below a shout. "After everything we've been through and everything this crew has seen you want us just to surrender and turn the ship over to a bunch of alien thugs? What's gotten into you?"

She smiled at him then answered, "I'm not asking you to surrender, I'm telling you." Before Marek could reply, she pulled a blaster from behind her back and fired in one smooth motion catching him square in the chest. He moaned as he dropped to the floor, his chest smoldering where the blaster had hit. Instantly she waved the blaster around the room freezing everyone in sight.

"You," She nodded towards the pilot, "Turn this ship around and get us back to Earth. Go directly to the facility where this ship was built. People will be awaiting its return to take charge of it. Do it, or you're going to join him in the afterlife."

Behind her the maglovator door opened, she spun towards the sound, pistol whipping into position to fire as a beefy fist launched out at her jaw, knocking her to the ground and unconscious in one blow. Her pistol clattered to the ground as the command crew sprang into action. General Abruzzi looked down at the young woman at his feet disdainfully as he rubbed his fist.

"Marek's alive." Wilson, the pilot shouted. "The uniform took the brunt of the blast."

"Get the Doctor up here." Abruzzi commanded authoritatively, "She's got a patient, and get this traitor down to the brig or whatever the hell you call it on this ship."

Two security personnel arrived a moment later and then stood silently above Reynolds holding blasters at her as she groggily began to awaken.

Abruzzi walked around tentatively and sat in the command chair. After he relaxed a moment within it, he smiled and said, "All right, you all listen up, this is what we're going to do..."

***

Back on Earth, in the underground catacombs, the rest of the Cagliostro's crew were not fairing any better than Mark or Ariel. Dan found himself suspended in an antigravity prison, where he was floating above the floor by energy that held him aloft there, unable to reach or touch anything solid. He cursed repeatedly under his breath and flexed his powerful muscles continually, but it was like he was trying to lift the planet. There was just too much mass arrayed against him. Dan merely grunted and redoubled his efforts.

Red Robinski was an extraordinarily tough man. The same aliens that had beaten Mark Johnson were finding that out as they hammered at him relentlessly with steel pipes across his ribs. He laughed, spitting out blood as he did, "Is that the best you salad heads can do?" He was untied, and being beaten by all three of the alien inquisitors. They were brutes who enjoyed their work, reveling in hurting the helpless and those who were weakened or that they had superior numbers against. It was three against one right now, and the three were hammering Red unmercifully. Finally he collapsed upon the floor, unmoving.

Eddie DiGenovese watched from a cell nearby as Red collapsed, and he gulped hard. The three jailers poked and prodded him for a few minutes, but he was not responding. Then one grabbed Red by the arm and began to drag him along the floor towards the cell they had previously thrown him and Eddie into.

"Oh man, Red…" Eddie whispered, wide-eyed and fearful, as Red's seemingly lifeless body was dragged closer and closer to the door.

One of the big purple aliens grunted and motioned Eddie away from the cell entrance, as the third one aimed his blaster at Eddie who raised his hands and backed up "Okay amigo, you're holding all the cards. Ol' Eddie is backin' away jus' like you wanted."

One of the aliens still held Red's limp, lifeless arm, while the other aimed the pistol at Eddie. The third began to punch in a sequence on the keypad next to the cell door, deactivating the laser beam bars that would cut a person to pieces before they realized it, if they had come in contact with them.

The instant the bars went off, the man holding Red's arm was suddenly hauled down as Red sprang upwards, driving his knee into the surprised salad head's jaws with all his considerable strength. The alien's neck cracked loudly as it broke and he went limp instantly.

The alien holding the gun spun on Red, surprised, when Red simply charged into him, with the dead alien held before him like a battering ram. At the same time Eddie charged through the open doorway and tackled the gun-wielding alien around the waist. Stunned, the alien dropped the gun, which Eddie snatched out of mid-air, spinning to one knee on the floor and firing two quick shots, one into the alien who was reaching for his pistol by the control pad where he had unlocked the laser doorway and the other into the alien he and Red had taken down just for good measure.

Eddie spun around warily looking up and down both ways in the prison-like corridor, as Red sank to the floor in a seated position.

"Red! You okay big man?"

"Not really Eddie. I think they broke a few ribs, but I'm not tasting blood, so hopefully nothings punctured." He turned towards Eddie, "These uniforms the boss created are a marvel. Without it I would be dead from that beating they gave me."

"Yeah, well amigo, we ain't outta the woods yet."
Eddie replied as he tossed Red a gun and then helped the
bigger man to his feet. Red grimaced and grunted as he
steadied himself.

"Now what?" Eddie asked.

"We find the boss, Ari and Dan. I gotta believe
everyone is down here somewhere."

"Did you try reachin' out with your mind? Seein' if Ari
picks up on us?"

"No Eddie, not yet. Let me give it a shot." Red closed
his eyes and concentrated a moment. Then opened them
and shook his head. "Nothing." I can't 'hear' any of them."

"Yeah me neither," the smaller man confirmed in a
barely audible whisper.

"Let's go," Red hissed, and began limping down the
well-lit hallway, with weapons drawn. They passed many
cells, all empty, all dark. Then, as they passed the last one
with its bars glowing brightly, but with no lights within, a
voice called out to them.

"You two gentlemen, hold it, please." A haggard, raspy
voice called out to them, with more than a hint of
desperation.

Both men went back towards the cell.

"Who's there?" asked Red.

A bedraggled man that they both instantly recognized
stepped forward from the shadows. His face wore a stubble
of many days, along with bruises. His shirt had more than
its fair share of blood stains and his hand was wrapped up
in a makeshift bandage made from one sleeve of his
tattered white shirt. Even so, he maintained his poise, and
held both shoulders steady and proud. "Hello gentlemen, I

cannot stress enough how good it is to see you both," the President said.

Chapter Twenty

"Hang on Mr. President, we'll have you out of here in a moment," Eddie offered immediately.

"The sooner the better, gentlemen," the bedraggled and battered President replied.

Red looked at the control panel, then turned back towards Eddie, "I don't know the code."

"Neither do I." Eddie replied, "Now get outta the way." He raised his pistol and fired at the doors control panel. Instantly the control panel exploded, showering the hallway with sparks. A half second later, all the cell doors that were active up and down the hallway went out. Above their heads the lights sputtered and failed as well.

"That was interesting," Red remarked as the President immediately got out of the now de-powered cell.

A hundred feet up the cell block, two figures staggered out into the dimly shining emergency lighting that had just shuddered to life, casting ghostly images upon the walls and cells of the hidden jail.

The two figures were obviously hurt, and were dragging their way towards the small group. One of the two held the other tightly and was helping that person walk.

"Mark!" Red exclaimed as he ran forward.

"Yes it's both Ariel and me. She's been hurt, hurry," he replied hoarsely. "We have to get out of here."

Mark dragged Ariel into the dim light. She smiled at their friends.

"Oh geeze, you both look like hell," Red exclaimed as he helped hold up Ariel.

"That's about how we feel too," Ariel grimaced as she wiped blood from her lips.

"Where's Dan?" Mark asked.

"Don't know," replied Red.

"Let's find him." Mark tapped the sleeve of his shirt, atop his wrist and a screen appeared on his sleeve. Mark tapped it twice more and it became an image of a grid with four red dots together in one square, but the fifth red dot was across the larger square the grid appeared in.

"That ain't good," Eddie mused aloud.

"Where are our weapons?" asked Red.

Mark tapped his sleeve in response once again and a handful of blue dots appeared, and close by.

"They're all at the end of this hallway, somewhere." he started, then continued, "now let's get them, then get Dan, and then get the hell out of here."

The group made its way to the end of the hallway, the only member of the group unhurt was Eddie, so he led the way.

Halfway to where the guns were hidden, at the end of the hallway, six of the purple skinned aliens appeared down the dim hallway and began firing their weapons at the escaping fugitives. Instantly Eddie dove to the floor, the pistol he had confiscated from the jailors they had overcome extended before him and firing before he hit the floor. Three quick shots fired, three of the enemy crumpled to the floor, lifeless.

Red fired the blaster he held, and another of the enemy thugs fell forward.

Mark raised his pistol simultaneously with the men beside him, pulled the trigger and nothing happened. Quickly he dove into an empty cell as a blaster bolt shot by from the opposite end of the hallway, barely missing his head. Mark slapped the gun along its battery pack a few times, but it was dead, either damaged or burned out. As he considered what to do, both Red and Eddie fired one after the other, followed by a thud at the other end of the hallway.

Mark didn't hesitate, and ran out into the hall once again, as his people followed him. Red helped Ariel, who clung to him while she rubbed her forehead with her free hand, obviously still pained.

"Good shooting boys." Mark congratulated them as they broke into the weapons cabinet and took back their property.

"You expected any less, Boss?" Eddie replied slyly.

Mark shrugged, and then grimaced immediately afterward in pain. "Right now I just want to get back to the Cag and let Dr. Troiano have her way with me." Mark replied painfully.

Ariel shot him a faux annoyed look before playfully slapping him on the back of the head. Then she grimaced from the pain that caused her.

"Okay," Mark began, "enough screwing around, let's go find Dan."

The group of five made a left and a quick right into another hallway. Mark followed the trail leading to Dan on his wrist scanner built into his uniform's sleeve, a small hologram played out across his sleeve showing a 3D image leading to Dan.

"How'd you get this layout?" Eddie asked, amazed at Mark's tech once again.

"I copied it from the base we were in on that desert planet. You know this is an exact copy of that underground base correct?"

Eddie nodded affirmatively, "Yeah boss, I know. Remember, I was there too."

Mark smiled, and then grimaced again in pain, "I know Eddie, let's get Dan."

Down the secondary hallway, which did not suffer the power failure as did the prison cell wing; another group of enemy guards appeared and began firing. Everyone dove for cover as blaster bolts flew overhead.

"I got this!" shouted Red, as he readied and primed his hand held cannon. Mark nodded and Red jumped into the hallway and fired his handheld cannon once then disappeared behind a wall extrusion on the opposite side of the hallway. A nano-second later there was an explosion at the far end of the hallway that shook the foundation beneath their feet with its power.

Mark raised his pistol to the side of his head, the barrel pointing up and peered out around the brick extrusion on his side of the hallway and saw nothing but dust and rubble. The air was filled with a choking fog of debris.

Ariel stepped forward before Mark could stop her, and placed her fingers to her temples peering down the hallway. "I'm not 'seeing' anything down there. I *think* they're all down."

Mark put his arm around her, steadying her, "Okay Ari, relax, you did well."

She smiled at him as she leaned into him, "Thanks boss," she said with a wink, "also I found Danny. He's this way."

"I knew where he was Ari," Mark replied, with a modicum of sarcasm. He pulled her close, making sure he supported her as she walked. "Red, you take point and keep that big gun up and charged, Eddie you stay behind Red to his left and down low, and I'll carry Ari. Dan should be right ahead of us."

"You sure you don't want me to take her, boss?" Red asked.

"No Red, we need your big gun, and your tactical mind to get us out of here. I'll take care of Ariel."

Red nodded, "Whatever you say, boss." Then he moved ahead of the rest with Eddie flanking him. They moved past the bodies of the men who had just tried to attack them, all were the purple skinned 'salad heads'.

Red looked at them and grunted as they squeezed past the mass of still steaming flesh the cannon had left. Red and Eddie motioned everyone to stay still as the two reconnoitered the area. Eddie leaned towards the bigger man and whispered, "Does this seem like déjà vu all over again to you, too?"

"Yeah shorty, been there, done that, again," Red answered with a lopsided grin as he and Eddie continued ahead.

The President had been silent until now as he stayed behind them all, walking guardedly with his newfound companions. "What's going on out there, Mark? What'd that alien spy do in my name?"

Mark turned to the President, then turned forward again looking ahead with his friends and teammates. "I wasn't sure if I had spoken to you or the imposter, sir." Mark began, "I assume there are ways of being sure you are who I want to believe you are. I was going to suggest testing you myself for DNA anomalies."

"Would that clear up any distrust you may have for me? Would it clear your mind that I was the real President Scaleia?"

"It would go far, Mr. President. It's something I can have my Doctor aboard the Cagliostro perform a simple test for that will tell us all who you really are with one hundred percent certainty."

The President looked to Johnson and nodded seriously, "Then let's do this DNA test as soon as we get aboard your ship and while we're on our way to the White House."

Mark furrowed his brow as he asked, "You want to go to Washington? We could be shot out of the sky before we ever arrived there."

"I'm, sorry Mark, but I don't just want to go there, I need to go there. A monster has not only my nation in the palm of his hands, but my wife and children held hostage there, too, and they don't even know it. They think it's me, their loving father and husband who is there with them right this very moment." The President clenched his fists in impotent rage, "That abomination of science is sitting on my sofa right now with its arm around my wife. That's something I will not allow." The President fairly growled while he clenched both of his fists.

Red returned to the two men after he and Eddie had walked to the end of the corridor and peered into the dimly lit room, "All clear, Boss-man." Red announced in a low voice.

"Good job, Red.

They moved as one, with the President behind them. He had insisted on carrying a weapon, him being a trained fighter and veteran of two wars himself. He held the pistol expertly as they entered the warehouse-like room in the underground base.

It was dark in this room. In fact the only illumination came from what was in the room's center.

In the center of the room stood a clear globe about nine feet in diameter, all around the globe were various controls and apparatus'. But what was held inside the globes center was what captured everyone's eyes. Dan Sledge hung suspended in the air inside the globe, by tendrils of energy. He could get no leverage against them nor put his great strength to bear in any way. He was trapped and helpless.

"We have to get him out of there," Mark announced as he moved forward into the very dimly lit room. He turned back and looked at the President, "Sir, stay back please. Let us handle this."

"Mark, I'm as much in this as you are. I have no intention of standing on the sidelines and watching you people put your lives on the line. I'm in with whatever you are planning here. Just get me home."

The group began to cautiously walk across the blackened warehouse-like space.

"I never thought I'd see Danny helpless," Eddie spoke aloud.

"After everything we've seen the last few weeks Eddie? Well there ain't nothin' that surprises me anymore." Red replied quietly as they cautiously walked together at the head of the pack, scanning the room around them.

"Be careful you two, I'm not reading anything on my hand scanner but they may have blocked them somehow."

Suddenly, Ariel grasped her head with both hands and doubled over moaning painfully.

"Ari!" Mark shouted as he caught her just before she fell to the floor.

Instantly the lights came on in the big facility. The five former captives looked around, as alien troopers surrounded them. In the midst of the troopers was the same uniformed alien who had captured them earlier. "I see you pathetic humans were trying to escape my hospitality. Now that's not a nice thing to do is it? You all should be thankful I have taken you in. Others would have simply shot you on sight."

"I don't know who you are, mister", the President shouted as he pushed his way in front of Mark and the others, "but I've had enough of you, your salad headed friends, and whatever evil you're planning for my planet and its people. We will defy you and further, we will defeat you."

"A noble speech, Mr. President, but one that is useless and, without teeth as it were. As for who I am, you may call me 'Klaxxus-17'and you may also call me 'Master'."

Chapter Twenty One

Mark and the others looked on in anger as Ariel stood there, leaning heavily on Mark, holding her head in abject agony. Ari looked up at Mark, tears of pain streaming down her beautiful face. "Q-quel." Was all she was able to stammer out between gritted teeth.

Mark looked around at this point, heedless of his own safety, while various alarms went off in his head warning him not to do anything. They were alarms he had every intention of ignoring.

While Eddie and Red had their weapons up and aimed at the aliens surrounding them, Mark had been holding Ariel up; otherwise she would have collapsed to the floor as if she had no skeletal structure. He leaned close to her and whispered, "I'm sorry," then placed her gently upon the floor before he pulled his weapon and in one smooth move aimed it directly at the head of Klaxxus-17. "Tell your people to stand down, now."

"Or what?" The bald headed purple skinned alien replied as he waved off his troops cautiously, "You'll shoot me? Please sir, consider that I am number seventeen in a series of clones. My eighteenth iteration will simply take my place."

"That may be so, Seventeen, but you will still feel a slow and painful death. I have no intention of simply disintegrating you. I'll shoot you once with the power set low enough to burn your brain from the inside out. It will be a building reaction that will be more painful for each instant it carries on. It will kill you, but it will feel like an eternity of pain searing behind your eyes. You'll be begging for it to end, and it seemingly won't. Eventually you will die, but it'll feel like an eternity by the time you do. In actuality it will be only minutes. You won't be able to tell the difference. You'll just be begging for death."

***

Behind everyone and forgotten in all of this, Dan Sledge continued to hang suspended in coruscating energy in the center of the great room.

Silently, Dan continued to strain against his bonds, his brow dripping sweat as he redoubled his efforts to tear free of the energy prison.

***

"A wonderful and frightening speech, Mark Johnson, but one I do not believe, for you see, you are less than an annoyance to me and my masters."

"This is a lot of energy and effort I'm standing in for 'less than an annoyance'. You people are planning something for my world, or you're afraid of us, which is what I surmised anyway. I may be wrong, but with the effort you've all put into this place, as well as creating another just like it back on the desert planet, I'd say you clowns are pretty well invested in this one."

"The name of my world is 'Duddas'. It is the sand world you speak of, and it is a beautiful place compared to this cold and green world of yours. There is too much water here, there is too much cold here. There are too many of you here." He pointed a finger at Mark, "and you are too dangerous to get off this world and out of this solar system to be allowed to bring your infectious madness to the rest of the universe. Best to obliterate you all, rather than to allow you to spread."

"Who are your masters? What world do they hail from?" The President barked.

"You do not ask the questions here, human, I do. Your title is meaningless in captivity. You are my prisoner. The only reason you are still alive is so that we can gather information from you for our invasion. Once we have all the security codes and any other necessary information needed to overcome your security systems you will be discarded."

The President began to raise his gun to shoot when Mark laid a hand on the weapon and stopped him.

"You talk a lot, Seventeen, but you've said nothing. What do you want here? Why all this subterfuge? If your masters wanted to destroy us, they could have done so from space."

"The masters know your weapons are great and powerful. You excel at destroying things. For some mad reason it is an art with your race. The universe knows this. A wary eye has been kept upon you for years."

"Like I told you before, I already surmised all of that already, Seventeen. There's more to it though isn't there?"

"Of course there is, human. Your race is to be crushed, enslaved and spread throughout the universe, never to gather as one people again. You are too dangerous, and your world's wealth will be broken up amongst the many races and distributed. Barbarians such as yourselves will never live free again. The Universal Emperor will see to that."

"The hell he will!" shouted the President as the blaster in his hand barked death and splattered the head, brains and blood of Seventeen all over his troops standing directly behind him.

"Aw, hell!" shouted Red, wide eyed as he immediately brought his weapon up and prepared to fire.

Instantly all about the crew of the Cagliostro weapons were raised and pointed at them as triggers began to squeeze.

But behind them, and all but forgotten, a powerful man strained to the breaking point and beyond, until with one more Herculean effort, Dan Sledge pulled against his ethereal bonds and this time he shattered them. The globe he was trapped in exploded outwards with a fury like unto an erupting volcano. Everyone in the room immediately looked towards the sound of his escape, including the Quell, who suddenly screamed as its concentration was shattered and Ariel put all her psychic strength, power and will into one pinpoint accurate bolt of psychokinetic retaliation, shattering the Quell's mind as his head snapped backwards agonizingly, blood instantly spraying from his eyes and nose, before he dropped to the floor, dead.

Now the troopers turned to fire at their enemies, but it was too late. Eddie was firing first, taking out half a dozen of the guards with almost super-human accuracy before any of them got a single shot off.

Red brought up his energy cannon as he dropped to one knee, resting the heavy weapon there as he fired. The sound was like standing next to a rocket at lift off, and the results were just as catastrophic, as the purple skinned guards were scattered across the warehouse-like room

Then Dan was there, leaping from across the empty room in one angry motion, landing the midst of their enemies, his powerful legs exploding downward into the concrete and steel reinforced floor, shattering it and sending shockwaves that scattered their enemies like tenpins.

Instantly the President, Red and Eddie took defensive positions behind crates that were scattered about the huge room and began firing as Mark joined them, having picked up a gun one of the enemy lettuce-heads had dropped, with Ariel hanging on to his shoulder for support.

The room was alive with bolts of energy flying every which way, as stunned guards tried to fight their way to their feet, but Dan would simply stomp on the floor with incredible strength sending shockwaves through the very ground, scattering them.

Ariel looked up and inhaled sharply, drawing in her breath. Then she turned to Mark and finally spoke, "I've got this," she stated with an almost feline growl as she walked away from Mark, put both hands on either side of her head and suddenly concentrated.

Every alien within the room suddenly dropped to the ground like puppets with their strings cut. Ari stumbled a second as blood began to run down from her nose, and Mark quickly caught her once again.

"I've got you Ari, I've got you," he reiterated reassuringly.

"We leavin'?" Dan asked as he rubbed his hands together, dispelling dust.

"Yes we are, Mr. Sledge," Mark replied as he tapped his sleeve, bringing up a 3D image of the cells and the entire underground compound. "This way," he stated flatly and pointed.

The entire team, including the President, began to run when suddenly the underground base shook violently.

"What the hell?" grunted Dan.

"We're under attack," Red shouted.

"Not us, this base," Eddied replied.

"Less talk, just run." Mark ordered, as everyone raced towards the staircase leading to the upper levels.

"Danny, take point and clear the way for us."

"You got it, Mark," Sledge replied as he barreled through half a dozen guards who suddenly appeared before them from an adjacent hallway. They were scattered and down before any of them drew a weapon as Dan Sledge tore through them like they were made of paper.

"Steel doorway to the outside ahead," Mark advised as they ran.

"Not for long," Red acknowledged as he brought up the cannon once again, "Danny, down!" Red yelled, as Dan hit the deck, barely avoiding a blast from the hand-held cannon which obliterated the bulkhead door, while the entire facility shook yet again from the continuing barrage from the outside.

"Everyone try to raise the ship, we have no idea how high up it is, or even where it is exactly. They could be doing this from orbit for all we know," Mark commanded.

"Not quite, Mark. Look!" Eddie shouted as he pointed above them.

The Cagliostro shot across the sky stopping almost directly overhead as a small hatch opened up on the bottom of the ship and a magnetic tractor beam grasped onto them all, drawing them into the ship.

Red and Dan each placed a hand on the Presidents upper arms, holding him lightly as they floated upward.

"How is this even possible? I have no metal on." The President stared in wonder as he floated upward.

"The beam is pulling you upward by the iron in your blood and whatever magnetic material is in our suits alone. It's that powerful, but it's also gentle. You're not feeling a tug or any pain. It's all calculated accordingly," Mark explained as they entered the ship through the belly hatch they were drawn up through.

Seconds later the entire group was running through the ship toward the forward maglovator and from there to the control deck.

They burst onto the control deck as the secondary crew all stood, all except the man in the command chair.

"You're all relieved people, good job," Mark began, but stopped when he saw the General sitting in his chair, "General, where's Mr. Marek?"

"In sick bay, Johnson. You had a traitor on board. She tried to kill your second in command, but I showed her the error of her ways," the General concluded, rubbing his fist ominously.

"Who was the traitor? Reynolds? From life sciences?"

The General raised his eyebrows in surprise, "Good instincts Johnson, yes that's the one. Pretty red haired tart too."

"Auburn sir, her hair color is auburn. I've been concerned about her since we got her back from that prison facility. According to the crew she made some comments on the Stargrazer that seemed a bit out of place for her. Where is she now?"

"The brig, nursing a black eye and one nasty headache I hear." He laughed quietly in memory of his arrival and subsequent knockout blow to the traitors jaw.

"Good, let her stay there and stew awhile." He turned to Ariel who was seated at her console, "You're going to the med bay, I'm taking you there myself. Mr. President, find a seat please."

At Mark's comment all on the command deck turned their heads suddenly to the maglovator doors, General Abruzzi included, who immediately stood and saluted the President.

"Mr. President! I apologize sir, I did not realize you were standing there," Abruzzi offered sincerely.

"At ease General, this is not a formal meeting. These people just saved my life. Believe me I'm not going to stand on circumstance at the moment. I've been in a cell for the past few weeks."

Then the President stopped, "Wait Abruzzi, what are you doing here?"

The General smiled slowly, "You were held the past several weeks sir, here. Johnson and his people found me thousands of light years from here held in an alien prison, where I'd been trapped for months or maybe even years. I guess we both owe them much," he concluded with a slow nod.

The President turned to Mark who was forcibly making Ariel leave her station and go with him to the medical bay.

"So I was correct, Mr. Johnson? We had a traitor in our midst, an imposter, besides the one who took my place?"

Mark nodded as the young woman who had taken Ariel's place at the communications console returned and did so once again. Mark led Ariel away. It was obvious she was still in pain from her ordeal. "Yes, Mr. President. You were right on all accounts. It was the General as we had surmised earlier who was replaced by the Aliens."

"Mark, get yourself looked at also, you look like hell, you know," the President stated.

"I feel like hell plus some," Mark replied, a slight grin in place.

"Danny, take the command chair, head to Washington. I'll be back in a few minutes. If attacked, don't fire on any of our own planes. Follow the Presidents orders."

Mark stopped a moment in thought as he looked at the view screen before him then turned back to Dan Sledge, "in fact belay that and head for orbit. Keep the reflective skin energized, Mr. President, please come with us, you too General. Red come with us and get yourself looked at."

"Mark," Red began, "I'm okay. Let me stay here while you're in the med bay. I'll go after you come back, is that okay with you?"

"All right, Red, I'll make sure you head down there the minute we're back on the deck, though. Mr. President, with us please?"

The President stopped and looked at Johnson quizzically, "What reason, Mark?"

"We have that little DNA test we were discussing earlier to administer. I think we all should take it to alleviate any doubts to everyone around us we are who we claim to be. Any of us who were captured by these aliens could have been cloned and replaced. Let's make sure the air is cleared and no one on board has doubts about any of us."

The General began to argue, but thought better of it and followed the President, Mark, and Ariel into the maglovator, exiting twenty seconds later in the medical bay.

Doctor, I have a couple of patients for you. First and foremost look to Ariel, then I need DNA tests administered to all of us, to make sure we're all who we claim to be, if anything, for the peace of mind of the crew."

"Never mind that, boss." Troiano began, "you look like hell yourself, get up on an exam table pronto."

"Ari first," Mark insisted.

Troiano shook her head disgustedly and heeded his wishes. Ariel painfully slid up onto the med gurney, wincing a few times as she did.

"Johnson, Abruzzi a moment please," the President called both men to his side.

"What is it Mr. President?" Mark asked as both men joined him in a corner of the medical facility.

"I have a thought as to how these DNA tests can serve two purposes. Let us have them performed on a live channel feed to the world. Can you do that?"

Mark thought a half second, then replied, "Yes we can bounce the signal off a satellite relay and blanket the world."

"Good. I can make an announcement about my imposter the instant the test is complete, and we can have both clones arrested on the spot."

"It may not be that easy, sir. It will be our word versus theirs and they could easily say a video DNA test was rigged."

"Perhaps, but it will instill doubt, and that could be all we need."

All three men agreed.

"Excuse me, Mark." The three men looked up as the doctor approached, her face serious, "I have Ariel stabilized. She's beat up, but nothing's broken. She needs rest. Now it's your turn, I need you on an exam table."

He nodded in agreement and turned back to the President and the General, "Gentlemen, if you'll excuse me, my Doctor needs to see me. The Doctor will need to see you too, Mr. President."

"That's right I will, so don't go anywhere, Mr. President." Troiano affirmed.

A nurse walked over and led the President to an examination table. The general stood quietly nearby watching, his face impassive.

"You were very lucky today, Mr. Johnson." Troiano began, "You all were. The med scanner doesn't show any breaks, just a lot of bruising. They held back on all of you."

He laughed and replied, "It didn't feel like it."

"Maybe not, but they didn't kill you."

"No they were torturing us, they wanted information."

He turned and looked at Ariel who was in the bed next to him, her eyes closed. "How is she, really?" He spoke in a lowered voice.

191

"She's hurting. They were brutal with her. She's scarred both mentally and physically. She needs to relax for a few days at least."

'*No!*' Ariel's voice shouted in both their minds, almost doubling them over with the strength of her psychic voice. '*I can rest after this is over with. The nation, hell, the planet needs us, all of us, myself included.*'

"Ari-" Mark interrupted.

'*No, no Mark, you will not put me on the sidelines for this one. I can take a nice long vacation after this is all over. For now the Doctor can medicate me or whatever. But I'm not sitting on the sidelines. I'm seeing this through to the end.*'

Johnson nodded finally after meeting her gaze for a moment. "Doc, fix her up. I do need her, we all do. She's right."

Troiano shook her head, "I must protest Mr. Johnson, she's my patient and she needs her rest."

"She can rest in her quarters until I need her, then I'll call for her. That's the only compromise I'm willing to make. You're both right, and you'll both have to sign onto it, whether you like it or not, especially you Ari. Doc, don't over medicate her, when the time comes I'll need her sharp. Literally the fate of the world may depend on it." He turned to Ariel now as both the President and General Abruzzi looked on in interest, "I'm not comfortable doing this Ari. But I do need you and I understand your desire to be in on the rest of this crazy mission we're on. But I will not allow you to be hurt again. If things start to look bad I'm pulling the plug and taking you out of the action, understood?"

Ariel sighed and nodded affirmatively. "Okay, I agree to your terms," she answered, exasperated.

"Good, now Doctor Troiano, there's a matter of DNA tests for myself, the General and President Scaleia. We have a broadcast to make to the world.

Chapter Twenty Two

Video equipment was quickly set up in the medical bay as the ships engineers, under Dan Sledge's attention, fed the video feed into the ships powerful communications array.

"We're all set, Mark," Dan called, as he plugged the final connection into the hovering camera, which floated about in front of the three men, while being controlled by Dan.

"All right Dan, thanks. Gentlemen, it's show time," he announced grimly.

"Lighting it all up in 3, 2, 1- You're live." Dan pointed towards them.

"People of the United States of America, as well as all of the Earth. My name is Mark Johnson. I'm sure in the past several weeks you have heard certain…disparaging rumors about me, and my friends and co-workers here at Johnson aerospace. I am here with President Scaleia as well as General Abruzzi, two of the most powerful men in the nation, and on the planet to dispel those rumors."

Sledge watched his control panel as the drone camera floated about the three men, concentrating its focus right now on Mark.

Its signal was being streamed off a Johnson Aero satellite and from there, sent all over the world hitting communications satellite after satellite. Even if their enemies shut some of the feeds down they would not be able to sever them all. Someone, somewhere of importance would see this message. At least that's what was hoped.

"We are here to prove to the American people as well as the world that we three are the real, true people we appear to be. You see, these two men beside me, President Scaleia and General Abruzzi, have both been captured by forces beyond our world and replaced with clones. We are going to do a live DNA test right now on the three of us to prove we are who we claim to be. Mr. President, you will be first."

The President nodded stoically and held his arm out as Dr. Troiano quickly took blood and then a culture from the inside of his mouth. She ran a scanner over them and the results were instantaneous. This was the real President according to information that was on file in the ships database.

"Next, General Abruzzi," Mark continued, "and after him I will be tested as well."

Troiano continued her testing on both remaining subjects with the same result each time.

Then it was the Presidents turn to speak, "My fellow Americans, the man sitting in the White House is not the man you elected. He is a clone of myself, a replacement programmed to destroy our great nation and even further, our great world. There has been a clandestine scheme enacted by an alien race to subjugate mankind. This is not some wild lame-brained tale by some discredited tab-feed. This is reality. Secret Service, I implore you to take the man in the White House into custody. I am calling on my three most trusted personal guards, Jenkins, Shlesinger, and Moroni. That man may wear my skin, but he does not wear my soul. His intentions are dire. Arrest him now, and do not hesitate to do so. I'm ordering the men who are with the imposter claiming to be General Abruzzi to do the same. Arrest him, do not let him escape custody. The fate of the world literally relies on you doing so."

Suddenly, Red's voice interrupted over the ships comm system, "They found us Mark, we have incoming, missiles headed our way, as well as two rapier class war ships."

"Destroy the missiles, full spread with the solar cannons, do not, I repeat do not fire on the war ships," Mark commanded.

The President continued, "This is not a lie, this is not desperate men trying to confuse or befuddle you. Even now the enemies of mankind fire upon us. I am the President of the United States of America, and I implore you to heed my words. The fate of the world's future is in your hands, and only you can assure that future. I can only guarantee that our world is lost if you do not heed my words at this very moment. Everything relies on what the people of Earth do within the next few scant minutes. This is our turning point as a planet, this is the moment we either climb to greatness, or are forced back into the mud by the boot heel of an enigmatic oppressor who fears us. Seize the future, seize it now, or there will not be a future, for any of us."

As he was speaking electronic data from the entire mission was being sent on every conceivable frequency across the world.

The ship rocked violently as the missiles shot at it were destroyed, but still they exploded powerfully and closely.

"We still have those rapier class ships incoming, Boss." Red barked over the comm.

"Are they arming weapons?"

"They have been armed, Mark."

"Continue broadcasting all vital information about this mission, loop it and send the damned information package to every receiver on the planet, I don't have to tell you to make sure it's all over the ultranet as well, I'm sure."

"Already done, boss," Dan replied.

"More missiles incoming!" Red snapped, the tension in his voice apparent. "Mark, there's waves of them heading toward us!"

"Fire at will, destroy them," Mark ordered as tension filled the ship, and was readily apparent over the video feed.

"Both those ships are moving on us now. They're trying to cut us off," Red shouted.

"Evasive maneuvers," Mark replied.

"Boss, should I keep transmitting?" Sledge asked.

"Yes, keep it going, I want the world to be watching this right up until our very last minutes if need be. The planet has to learn we are who we say we are and the extent of the trouble that's coming to us."

"Those ships are flanking us now and are powering up their weapons."

"Shields to full!" Mark shouted.

"They're firing!" Red yelled over the comm.

Then the ship shook slightly as if it was riding a wave, a particularly nasty one, but a wave nonetheless. But nothing beyond that occurred.

"What was that? What just happened?" Mark asked cautiously.

An instant later Red replied, "Those two rapier class ships, they shot the missiles out of space and blocked us with their own hulls, I have Captain Tadeo of the 'Samson' on the comm requesting to speak to you now, sir."

"I'm on my way to the command deck, Red." A relieved Mark turned towards Abruzzi and the President, "Gentlemen, if you'll follow me?"

Minutes later Mark, Dan, the President and General Abruzzi all entered the command deck from the maglovator. On the view screen was the image of Captain Tadeo, a man of indiscriminate Asian ancestry. The Captain immediately stood and saluted when he saw the President and General follow Mark onto the command deck.

"Mr. President, General Abruzzi, sirs. So good to see you both."

"At ease, Captain," the President spoke, "This crew and this man, Captain Mark Johnson, saved both our lives on a mission I sent him on several weeks ago. I was taken out of the White house in the dead of night by aliens who had built a secret base in the midst of the Blue Ridge mountain range."

"I have already forwarded those coordinates with the information package," Mark interjected.

"And we have them, thank you Mr. Johnson." Tadeo replied. "Right now the imposter President has been taken into custody and is undergoing DNA Scans as we speak, to verify your claims sir. I'm positive they will prove you to be the real President of the United States. The General's imposter has not been found as of yet, he slipped away when your transmission began, but there are men searching for him right now."

"Do not let that man get away, he has vital information we will need." The president ordered.

"What about that damned base in the midst of our nation and so close to our capitol?" Abruzzi asked.

"According to the people on the ground, it looked like it took a pounding recently I assume that was your people?" Tadeo asked.

"Yes," Mark affirmed, "we broke out of there earlier after being held captive ourselves. Any enemies found within its walls?"

"Not as of yet, it looks to be abandoned according to the information I am reading." Tadeo replied.

"They cut and ran, but to where I wonder?" Mark rubbed his chin in thought.

"It could be anywhere, chances are they left the planet already," the General offered.

"True, General. I'll be taking the Cagliostro down into Washington, I want to drop the President and you off as close to the White house as possible."

"I will gladly send two fighters down with you to escort you in." Then the Captain added, "That is one tough ship you have Mr. Johnson."

"Thank you Captain Tadeo," Mark replied, saluting. Tadeo returned the salute solemnly then did likewise to the General and the President before saying good-bye and cutting off his communication.

Johnson turned towards the President, "I have to ask sir, why did you tell Tadeo I was the Captain of this ship? I have no official designation. I own her and built her but in that regard only am I her Captain."

"That's not true any longer, Mr. Johnson. As of now you have a special dispensation from the highest office in the land. Mine. As of this minute, officially you are Captain of this ship in name, and rank as well as every other way shape and form you have already demonstrated. When this is over you will receive an official commendation noting it as well, providing we survive all of this."

Mark smiled as a look of surprise covered his face, but he worked well at hiding it after only a second or two.

"Thank you, Mr. President," Mark solemnly replied.

"No, Mr. Johnson, Thank you. Without your foresight and thought I would still be trapped in the secret facility that was built on American soil by an alien race." He thought for a second more then added, "What I want to know is how they managed to build an entire base right under our noses without any of us being the wiser?"

"I have more than a few ideas on that, Mr. President."

"There's time for that later. Can you return me directly to the White House?"

"Post-haste Mr. President, Post-haste."

***

Five minutes later, still smoldering from re-entry, the Cagliostro set down gently upon the south lawn of the White House. The Star fighters that escorted the Cag flew overhead in a patriotic 'fly by'.

President Scaleia exited the Cagliostro a moment after its foot ramp touched down, with Mark at his side.

"Mr. Johnson, it has been a pleasure, you are a patriot as well as a brilliant engineer, and I thank you for rescuing myself and General Abruzzi from these alien terrorists."

"I did exactly what anyone else in my position would have been willing to do, Mr. President." The two men shook hands, "I'll drop off General Abruzzi in Arizona, where he can see to his command," Mark commented.

"Very good, Mr. Johnson. Fly safely." The President turned to walk into the White House as the guards and secret service agents filling the White House lawn looked on impassively, then he stopped and turned back towards Mark, "I have to amend that, not Mr. Johnson, but Captain Johnson."

Johnson stoically saluted as the President returned the salute, spun on his heel and walked up the front steps of the White House his guards following him in.

Mark relaxed for a moment as he walked up the ramp of the Cag and pensively looked down its gleaming thousand-foot length. Then he continued inside.

A moment later the ship was airborne and streaking towards Arizona.

"What's our ETA at current speed?"

"One hour, Captain." Red smirked, "though I could speed it up and have us there in a few seconds at most while in the atmosphere."

"Very good, Mr. Robinski, but I think an hour sounds better. We've been running around the universe for weeks. Let's take our time on the last leg of the trip, now that we've got some semblance of control back in our lives, at least for the moment. I'll be in my quarters." He turned toward his communication officer and spoke, "Ariel, you need to rest. C'mon, time to stand down," he beckoned to her to join him. Ariel stood and walked to his side leaning on him for support, as she was still shaky from her ordeal hours earlier.

Once on the living quarter's deck, the couple exited the maglovator and entered Mark's quarters, as the door hissed shut behind them.

***

Moments later they were both lying back on his bed, Mark holding her comfortingly.

"Are you sure you're okay?" he asked her quietly.

"I'm hurting, Mark. Let's not ever do that again, okay?" He touched the black and blue on her jaw and she winced slightly at his touch.

"Sorry," he consoled.

"I know. It's part of the game, I get that. I just don't know if I'm built for this game. I-I've never been hit like that before, in my life I mean."

Mark sighed sadly, "I know you are hurt, I really want you to take time off from all of this when we get home. Relax for a week or two. Then we can decide on a new position for you"

"Mark, none of this is over, you know that. Not yet. You need me right now. After this is over I'll gladly take a vacation. We're going to war; you know I'm not telling you anything you don't already know."

"Ari, you have to understand, I just saw the results of you being beaten badly. It's not anything I ever want to see again."

She pushed herself up on an elbow and looked at him, "Mark, I know you're worried about me, but right now you have to be more concerned with what we—the entire planet is facing. I'll be all right. But everyone else needs you more than I do right now. This doesn't mean when all this is over that I won't want to take a nice desk job at headquarters, but I have to say, beyond the getting socked in the jaw part, I think I'd end up missing all of this." She waved her hand up in the air, indicating space.

Mark shook his head, looked away and exhaled before turning back to her and answering, "You are one confusing and infuriating woman."

"Aren't we all?" she smiled demurely, and shrugged her shoulders with a smile.

Chapter Twenty Three

The Cagliostro hovered in place then slowly began to enter the cavernous hanger before it. The ship settled in and quietly powered down. Across a loud speaker in the bustling hanger, a woman's voice spoke, "Maintenance crew to hanger thirteen, repeat, maintenance crew to hanger thirteen, full diagnostics and repair crews required as well.

The boarding ramp touched down and people began streaming out of the ship instantly, Mark at the forefront. "I want full diagnostics on shield data downloaded to me personally. I want weapons diagnostics as well. Weapons power and efficiency must be increased by at least one hundred percent."

Red grasped Mark by the arm.

"Hold on Mark, one hundred percent? You want to double weapons power? How are you going to do that? We could be attacked at any minute for all we know."

"We won't be. They may be out there, Red, but they have a healthy respect of us now. Maybe even a fear, if we're lucky. That's something we can play on."

"Okay, fine, but is the ship going to have the structural integrity to withstand you doubling weapons output?"

"Red, c'mon, it's me. I have so much redundancy built into the Cagliostro that it could withstand five times the stress I'm going to subject it to."

"I hope you're right, boss, no matter what we've just been through the past few weeks, this is still an experimental ship. Meaning anything could blow up in our faces at any time."

"No Red, not true. This ship is rock solid. Besides, I was having new weaponry developed while we were gone. Advancements were being made based on our data that we were broadcasting back to headquarters the entire time we were out there. New and vastly improved solar cannons are going to be fitted before the day is over. Shield generator capacities are being doubled so their energy siphoning device won't work on us any longer."

"Wait a sec; I thought we had already beaten that trick of theirs?"

Mark smirked, "Not at all Red. In order to defeat those siphoning beams of theirs I had Abruzzi powering up every shuttle ship in the landing bay and adding its energies to the Cag's."

"Ha!" Red guffawed, "I meant to ask you about that. I figured you just had some brainstorm idea pop outta your head and you beat that trick of theirs that way."

"What? You don't think my idea of adding energy from the shuttles to the Cag's was a brilliant idea? I thought it was myself, actually."

"I'm sure it was, boss. You know engineering ain't exactly my thing."

Mark waved Red off, "It's okay Red, don't sweat it I'm just playing with you a little. Now we have to get some rest, all of us."

"Are you going home?" Red asked.

"No, I figure I'll sleep aboard ship. I don't want to leave her unguarded."

"Hey if you're going to stay, so am I. I'll leave a security detail aboard with us just in case. If they see anything ...questionable they'll contact us immediately."

Mark shook his head, "No Red, if they see anything tell them to shoot first and ask questions later. Right now, until those engines are manufactured and ready to be mounted on our fleet within the solar system, we are standing in front of the fastest ship on the planet. That's a tactical advantage we cannot lose."

"Did you look into how close those other engines are to being completed?"

"Yes, as we were on approach I put a call in. We're still at least two days away for the first set. The second set is at least a week away."

"That ain't good," Red replied.

"None of it is," Mark reaffirmed. "We're in trouble in that we can't take a full scale assault back to these guys. Hell, we know so little about them; the first question should be where do we go to find them?"

Dan and Eddie walked up and joined Mark and Red.

"How are you both doing?" Mark asked.

"Alright boss." Eddie nodded affirmatively.

"The ship all settled in Dan?"

"Yeah boss it is. She's good."

"Where's Ari?" Eddie asked.

"I had her stay aboard with Dr. Troiano looking after her. That salad headed bastard did a number on her. " He flexed his fists involuntarily as he thought about Ariel's bloodied and bruised face.

"Nothin' you can do about it now boss, the guy's dead. Everyone in that hole in the grounds gotta be after what we put 'em through." Dan replied as the men entered a door heading towards the offices within the huge hanger.

"Is security in place around the facility, Red?"

"Yes I questioned the security head before we landed. I wanted to make sure everything was in place and locked down."

"Good. I was worried about that," Mark answered.

"Since when do you worry about anything?" Dan asked, wide eyed.

"This adventure taught me a lot, my friends. This universe is a much larger place than we ever realized. We always knew we were not alone, at least for a long time. But whatever evidence we had paled in comparison with the incontrovertible proof we discovered within a few days of leaving Earth."

Dan shrugged his big shoulders, "Yeah boss, you got that right at least. I don't think any of us were ready for such a hot reception when we got to that desert planet. Duddas, I think Seventeen called it before the President blew his brains out."

"Yeah that was a hell of a thing wasn't it?" Dan remembered.

"This entire mission was a hell of a thing so far," Eddie replied.

"Ain't that the truth." Red answered.

"Boss, do you want us to stay aboard tonight? Just you know, in case?" Dan asked protectively.

"No, you two go home, relax. Tomorrow we have to get the Cag outfitted with the improvements that we want implemented; in fact Dan, you and I have some design work to do ahead of us. I've already got a few ideas to boost things up in both shields and solar cannon strength, even beyond what is being mounted in the coming days."

"Me too, Boss."

"Okay Dan, get home and get your feet up, relax for tonight I'll see you in the AM. Try not to be here too late."

"Ya know boss, I think I'm just gonna stay on board. I can get home tomorrow some time. Tonight, well I got a bad feelin' about this."

Red turned towards Dan and grinned wolfishly, "So I'm not the only one eh?"

"You too?" Dan asked grimly.

"Yes, me too. Something is just not right."

"And I thought it was just me." Mark confided, "If you two are going to stay on board then let's get back on there now. I have to see Dr. Troiano about Ariel."

Eddie shrugged his shoulders, "I might as well stay too then, not like I have anyone waitin' at home for me." And then added after a moment, "An Troiano ain't exactly hard on the eyes." he added with a grin.

Mark smirked as he began walking up the boarding ramp, "Good let's get inside and kick back a little while."

"Good? Whattaya mean good? I ain't got no life a my own away from this place, you should be feelin' sorry for me!" Dan's voice trailed off as they entered the ship.

Eddie replied with a laugh, "Feel sorry for you? Do I feel sorry for the orangutan in the zoo because he's in a cage?"

"Hey! Watch yer mouth scrawny before I pop yer head off yer shoulders like I was openin' a Pez dispenser."

Their voices trailed off within the ship as they disappeared from its entry way.

***

But unseen by all, near a skid of barrels, something dark and mysterious stirred. It moved cautiously through the darkened hanger bay, a bay designed only for the Cagliostro. It skulked within the shadows awaiting those who still loitered within the cavernous expanse to leave for the evening as technicians finished up their duties on the great ship and began to filter out of the huge building.

Finally, after several more hours of skulking about and keeping to shadows the hanger was mostly empty, at least as empty as the shadowy being deemed it would ever get. Its impatience was beginning to gnaw at it like unto a dog with a bone as it crept stealthily towards the boarding ramp of the Cagliostro, under its gleaming, majestic bow.

The creature crept on all fours, cautiously watching as it swept its shadowy head from side to side. Up the ramp it crawled on all fours, its long, thin tongue slashing forward to test the air ahead of it like a snake.

Suddenly its head snapped around, revealing a serpentine face of absolute blackness as reptilian eyes dilated in surprise as a voice caught its attention entering the hanger.

"Damned keys, where the hell'd I leave them?" The technician muttered with his head down as he made a beeline to his work bench and began rummaging through it frantically. He never saw the night dark thing silently slide up behind him, never felt its presence until its hand was around his neck and then he was dead, his neck snapped like a twig, as the creature now carried the dead tech like a feather. Then cautiously looking about, dumped the man's body into an empty barrel, before forcing a lid back upon the top, and returning to the ramp, disappearing into the ship with one last surreptitious look around.

***

Within the ship, Mark stopped in at the sick bay, where Dr. Troiano and her team of doctors were checking up on those on the ship that still needed care. Matt Marek was in a hospital bed in one of the small rooms off of the sick bay scrolling through a video feed. He had broken several ribs when he was shot almost point blank by the mad woman, Reynolds, but his uniform had absorbed not only the energy component of the blast, but much of the impact as well. Mark knocked on the open door as he walked in, "How are you feeling, Mr. Marek?" Mark asked.

"Hey Boss, I was shot, how do you think I feel?" He grinned.

"Ummm probably like you had a bulls-eye on your chest?"

"Haha- oww. Don't make me laugh, boss. That hurt." Marek moaned.

Johnson chuckled as he exited the room, "Get some rest, Mr. Marek, I'm sure I'm going to need you soon."

"I'll be ready boss." Matt Marek called after Johnson as Mark walked towards another room on the hospital level. Neither man mentioned the loss of Miles Jefferson, who was the second team commander before Marek, until he perished a short week and a half ago, along with forty other crewmen. But it was on both their minds.

Mark rapped his knuckles on the door of another room and walked in as Dr. Troiano turned at the sound of him entering. In the bed she was attending to was Ariel.

"How is the patient, Doctor?"

"How do you think, Captain? She's stubborn and rude."

"I am not!"

"Yes, you are young lady, and it's not your most endearing quality, let me tell you that much at least."

"Whoa, what'd I walk in on ladies?" Mark asked with his hands held out before him.

"She's insisting she wants to go back to her quarters. Now that we're on the ground I'd like to keep a closer track of her injuries, and she's fighting me on it. I was trying to…suggest… that she stay here tonight where there will be a Doctor on duty all night, myself actually, so I can make sure she's not having any repercussions after that beating she took yesterday."

"Ari, that's actually a very good idea," Mark began, before she cut him off with a motion of her hand.

"Like hell it is, Mister! I got a little banged up, that's it. I feel fine now, you and Dr. Troiano here are making more out of this then it is. You're like a couple of mother hens."

"C'mon Ariel, you know that's just not true—" he began, before she cut him off again.

"Mark Johnson, don't you dare try that condescending crap with me. I know what you're trying to do and it won't work. I want out of here and I want to go back to my own quarters, and you and I have been together long enough that you know I'm going to get my way once I set my mind to it."

"That may be so, Ari, but I could always have Dr. Troiano deem you unfit for duty, and have you medically confined to this medical bay. How would that make you feel?"

"You wouldn't dare," she snapped.

"Don't push me Ariel. I have a lot to consider here, including the wellbeing of the entire planet. We have aliens out there who are gunning for us, the whole Earth, and we don't even know who they are yet. But they are out there, I have to help outfit the Cag tomorrow with next generation weaponry and shield generators, plus I have a feeling I'm going to hear from the President as well. I don't need to add you to my concerns."

She visibly deflated. "All right, I'm sorry I was acting like an idiot."

Johnson eyed her, and he realized he really was annoyed with her at the moment. He turned back to Dr. Troiano and asked, "What do you think? She already sat on the command deck through all of that and helped out there, and she slept in her bed last night. Is she okay?"

"I'm sure she is Mark, but I'd really like to just get one night of observation in on her."

"I really do feel okay." Ariel reiterated, this time a lot more docilely.

"Look, let's just let her stay in her room tonight and tomorrow I may have to fly to Washington, at least that's what I'm assuming is going to happen. If I do, I'll take the Stargrazer while the Cag gets refitted. She will report back here at 0900 tomorrow, guaranteed. Whoever is on can watch over her then. Is that okay with you?"

Troiano sighed and shook her head, "All right. Take her. But if she exhibits any signs of trauma or anything else that you would consider odd, you call me and I'll get her back in here on an anti-grav gurney faster than you could say 'admitted'."

Mark nodded grimly, "Absolutely." he agreed with Dr. Troiano.

"Good, now go, both of you. Get out of my medical bay, and nothing strenuous. You both know what I mean," she called after them as they exited the medical bay and entered the maglovator.

"That wasn't fun," Ariel murmured.

"No it wasn't, and that wasn't the Doctor's fault. What's the matter with you? She just wanted to look after you for a night to make sure you didn't have a concussion or something she missed the first time around."

"I-I know, but you know how I hate hospitals."

"Ari, this is not exactly 'Mercy General'. This is a small ship, with a finite number of crew and medical staff. It wouldn't have hurt you to stay a night under the Doctor's care."

She put her arms around his neck and looked up at him with her big blue eyes, "Aww but I wanted to stay with my Captain tonight," she answered playfully.

She leaned upwards and kissed him, and he returned her kiss.

"This doesn't excuse you from spending tomorrow with Troiano. I want her to look after you," he admonished sternly.

They exited the maglovator and headed towards his quarters.

"Stay in my quarters tonight, I want to be near you."

She shook her head and immediately had a disgusted look on her face, "Seriously Mark, all kidding aside, you really are mother henning me you know."

"Go on get inside, and get ready to go to sleep." He grunted as he opened the double door with a wave of his hand in front of the palm reader on the door's edge.

The instant they entered the darkened room, Ariel knew immediately that something was wrong.

"Mark!" She turned and shouted as a dark figure that blended in perfectly with the pitch black of the room tackled Johnson and sent him sprawling into the darkness.

Chapter Twenty Four

Ariel screamed as Mark rolled away with whatever was atop him in the dark room. She hit the wall panel repeatedly for the ship wide communication web as well as the lighting control, but nothing worked.

Meanwhile Mark rolled to avoid getting clawed by his adversary, who hissed and spit repeatedly at him. Claws raked his shoulder and he let out a grunt before he finally unfolded a right cross to where the things head should have been. He impacted with…something. It felt like some kind of jaw, but definitely not human.

He began hitting it repeatedly as Ariel stood just within the doorway, unsure of what to do. She placed her hands upon the sides of her head and began to concentrate, but what her mind felt when it reached out and touched the thing that was trying to kill her lover was a mind of something other than human. It was almost all predator and it was thrilled with the hunt. The battle it now fought seemed to bring the vile thing glee.

Ariel tried to invade its mind, to hurt it psychically, but to no avail. It ignored her, as if its brain was not evolved enough to notice what she was doing to it. She reached for her blaster, which hung by her belt, but was afraid to use it for fear of hitting Mark.

Meanwhile the man so much hope and need rested upon continued to fight for his life. The beast slashed towards his throat, but somehow, his vision adjusting to the dark, Mark saw it coming as he swung his upper body away from his attacker, who merely scratched the floor. Mark swung a quick right cross to the side of its jaw and spun it sideways, then he hit it again, and twisted its body off of him as he did.

Mark scuttled away, getting to his feet quickly as the seemingly feral creature leaped at him again. This time, Johnson was ready; he sidestepped and parried the beast's outstretched hands, shoving it off balance as it passed by him so it landed in a heap against the wall.

Almost instantly the thing was on its feet again, as the room suddenly blazed to fully lit from complete darkness. The creature was horrific, a true unearthly beast. It was jet black and shiny, with skin like armor. Long talons and slavering reptilian jaws along with a jagged bone-like tail completed the picture.

Standing in the doorway now was not just Ariel, but Dan, Red and Eddie. The beast saw them and hissed loudly as it bent closer to the floor. Then it quickly leaped toward Mark once again, claws outstretched, but before it could cover the few feet between them blaster bolts rang out from the opened doorway. Three in total, Eddie fired first then Red and finally Dan. Each shot was close upon the other and all three hit their mark. The monstrosity fell to the carpet, and lay there steaming through three holes in its chest.

"What the hell is that thing?" Eddie shouted.

"Eddie, I have no idea. I want to know how it got in here in the first place though."

Red and Dan walked over to the creature and poked it with their feet, while they held their guns upon it.

"Well it's dead now, whatever it was," Red confirmed.

"Yeah, I kinda got that." Mark replied sarcastically as Ari moved to help him wipe up his blood from his shoulder wound and the scratches he had suffered at the beast's claws.

Ari then tapped her right sleeve and spoke, "Medical emergency, Mark Johnson's quarters."

Troiano's voice replied, "On my way."

"Hey boss," Dan suddenly spoke, alarm weaving its way into his voice, "you better take a look at this."

Mark moved past Ariel, who followed him back to the side of the room where the creature lie, and he stopped short, his eyes now as wide as Dan and Red's. Eddie still stood by the door, guarding in case the creature had a partner.

As the three men and Ariel looked on, the creatures form began to shimmer and almost melt before their eyes. Jaws dropped in unison as it began to shift into a familiar form.

"General Abruzzi?" Mark exclaimed in surprise. But then its flesh flowed once again, back into the nightmare creature it was, before finally melting into a puddle of gelatinous goo at their feet.

"Well I guess you two ain't stayin' in here tonight," Eddie murmured.

"Now we know what happened to the General's imposter. It was never a clone at all; it was a shape shifter of some kind."

"Whatever it was that thing stinks." Red complained as he covered his face and backed away from the still quivering puddle.

"Ugghh, it smells terrible." Ariel agreed as they all moved into the hallway.

Mark touched his sleeve, "I need a security team, life sciences in hazmat gear, as well as maintenance, to my quarters immediately."

Dan looked into the room and shook his head, "It's gonna be a long night. You shoulda told those guys to bring clothes pins for their noses too."

***

Twelve hours later, the Stargrazer landed in Washington, D.C. Mark, Dan and General Abruzzi exited the ship and were hustled off to a meeting in the Pentagon, one that was being broadcast to every civilized nation on Earth.

Mark, Dan and the General entered the meeting chamber, a circular room with a matching meeting table at its center. Already seated were the President and Vice President, along with certain congressmen, senators, generals and other high-ranking officials.

"Mr. President, senior staff members." Mark began, nodding as he entered the room with Dan and Abruzzi a half step behind him. Abruzzi saluted.

"General, Captain Johnson, Mr. Sledge." the President answered.

Mark paused a moment then began to speak, "You have all been briefed, so I won't waste any of your time recounting my mission to a galaxy an almost incalculable distance away from here. But the fact stands that not only did we find General Abruzzi there, the real General Abruzzi, we also found a shape shifting…thing had taken his place and then tried to murder me aboard my own ship last evening. The real General was held captive as I'm sure you all know by now, for at least several months, to as many as three years. Now since neither he nor I have slept much in the last forty eight hours we both need to make our points and do so quickly."

Around the table men looked to each other and began to murmur amongst themselves. Johnson allowed this for a few seconds before he cleared his throat to get their attention. "Gentlemen, please, time is of the essence here. We cannot waste what we have of it arguing amongst ourselves. Whether any of you in this room or watching around the globe realize it, we are about to go to war, and for the first time it is not with one another. Aliens are coming for us, one and all. Beings from a galaxy that we could never reach were it not for my magno-disc engines."

"So are you saying it is your fault they are here and coming for us?" a senator from Massachusetts shouted suddenly.

"No senator, they are coming here because they know we pose a threat to them, if we ever get out of our own solar system that is."

Another senator, this time from New York asked, "What are you talking about?"

"I'm talking about the end of the world, gentlemen. Life as we know it is about to end. And whether we are on the victor's side of this war or the losers is up to us as a world. These aliens, of which I have only met, what I would term as the workers or foot soldiers, so far, are a purple skinned race with hair that appears to be very much like lettuce. Hence my people have begun to refer to them as 'Salad Heads', and what these salad heads want is to subjugate our world."

"But why?" a congressman from South Dakota asked, incredulously.

"The answer, sir, is simple, they fear us. They fear our technology as well as our supposed bloodthirstiness. They seem to fear our ability to make weapons beyond our space faring ability. But beyond that, I have to assume they want to strip mine our planet and turn our survivor's into slaves, which is what I was pretty much informed of. This is no joke, distinguished sirs. They are coming here; the only question is when and how."

"What do you mean 'how'?" one of the senators asked.

"By how I mean are they coming en masse? Or as they have up until now, surreptitiously."

"How long do you believe they've been hidden here, Johnson? I've read your report and saw your vid-feed yesterday. What is your first hand assessment?" an Admiral asked.

"Admiral, they have been here for years. In fact if you turn to page forty six of your briefing report, you will see the information we have been able to gather over the past two days about the base my crew managed to destroy under the Blue Ridge Mountain range in Virginia."

"This is insane!" The Vice-President leapt upwards, and exclaimed excitedly, "Do you mean to tell me we have had an alien race living under our noses, mere miles from the capitol of this nation? I've read your report, but I find it farfetched and unbelievable to be honest."

"Whether you believe me or not, they were living here Mr. Vice-President, but they were here for a reason, to spy on us. To keep tabs on us, and to undermine our space program. They did not want us to reach for the stars. I have to assume they came to our world after our nascent space program reached the moon over a hundred years ago. They watched us and I'm sure they sabotaged our space programs around the world since they arrived here, whoever they truly are."

One congressman got to his feet to interrupt. He waved a flabby hand, which set his many chins flapping as the light within the chamber reflected off his gleaming bald head. "I find this all very hard to believe," the congressman began with a southern drawl. "Do you mean to tell me that an alien race has nothing better to do then keep tabs on us? A race that must be small and insignificant to them by a space faring and technological standard? Why would they bother with us? What harm could we possibly do to them? How would we even know of their existence?"

"I can answer that," the President turned and faced the congressman, "The Hubble V tele-satellite in orbit around Pluto was taking deep space photographs when it saw something that at first our top men thought was a simple comet, or rather a group of them, all exiting an unnamed solar system incredibly far from here. Only after several of the top men in many different scientific fields had examined the photographs did we realize what they were. In fact if not for Mr. Johnson's expertise we would still be scratching our collective head over this one."

"Yes," Mark chuckled slightly, "this was something we should have realized, but being the scientists that we were, we completely ignored the obvious. It was in fact, too much for our small minds and fragile psyches to consider. For the very first time we would have to seriously acknowledge we were not alone in the universe."

"Get to the point Johnson," the same congressman coughed again.

"Very well, we had witnessed a fleet of ships leaving a solar system, and traveling faster than light. They appeared to be streaking celestial bodies, meteors or comets, but in truth they were great star spanning vessels, a fleet of them, and the only reason I was able to ascertain this was that their rate of speed, based on what we were able to see, did not compute. They were so far away that they should have appeared to be barely moving. Instead their great streaks of light across the star speckled backdrop of the universe actually brought them to our attention."

"Yes, and when this information was brought to my attention I knew we as American's, and as Earthmen, had to discover what was out there as quickly as possible, for the sake of everyone on this planet," the President finished.

"Which is why the President sent my crew and I on a secret mission to a world we had pinpointed a lot of activity coming and going from."

"This is all too fantastic to be real," the Vice President shook his head and spoke almost to himself as he looked away. "You mean to tell me, Salvatore, that you sent these men away on a matter of national security and you couldn't even inform me of it?" He whined, his voice gradually growing higher in pitch as his anger grew."

"Stand down, Todd," President Scaleia ordered sternly, "These people saved my life as well as General Abruzzi's. From now on they have carte blanche as far as I'm concerned."

The vice president huffed and puffed, throwing his chest out as he paced around his seat, before finally sitting back down.

Mark instantly seized the moment, "This is not the time to fight amongst ourselves. This goes for all of you watching around the world also. Now the time has come for all of mankind to act as brothers, as family, to defend our world. If you want to go back to killing each other when all of this is over and done I sure as hell won't try to stop you. But for now we have to work together, otherwise life on this big blue marble is over."

"But what can we do?" A voice coming over the monitor said with an Indian accent.

"That part is simple," Mark began as he flipped a switch on the table in front of him, activating a holographic display that sprang to life in the center of the room. In the display was the schematic for a new type of engine, the magno-disc engines that powered the Cagliostro and the Stargrazer both. "We build these, on double shifts around the globe building and outfitting every damned ship we can find with them. And once that's done we take the fight to them."

"That sounds all well and good, Mr. Johnson, but for all we know they could be here right now, and from what I see, it will take months, perhaps years to ready our fleet of ships for deep space travel," a senator from Maine replied.

"You are correct sir, it will take years at the earliest to have the new engines installed in our entire fleet. But the few that are on hand and ready to be installed will be our first step in the right direction. You see, esteemed sirs, we do not need to leave the solar system to defend ourselves, we merely have to be able to fight off any attacker who comes to us, meaning to do us harm as a nation and as a world. I can help in both regards. I can re-arm our ships with the most advanced weaponry we have ever developed and I can continue to have the new magno-disc engines readied for installation on whatever ships you deem ready to go interstellar. But make no mistake gentlemen. The enemy is coming for us, and it is not to shake hands. It is to bury us so deep that the universe will forget it ever heard the word 'Earth', or the term 'human'."

Chapter Twenty Five

The work began around the clock at every Johnson Aerospace factory across the country as designs were pounded out and refined, allowing the first ships to be refitted. Mark Johnson himself oversaw the first re-fits aboard the Cagliostro, as the Cag flew parts to ships in orbit, where the war ships were flown into the huge hangers attached to the many space stations that orbited the Earth.

The ships would fly into the hangers, doors would seal, force fields would activate and the hangers would flood with oxygen, where technicians would work in space suits, but with their helmets open, ready at an instants notice to close the suits up in case of emergency. Working in zero-g allowed the technicians the ability to handle multi ton units without actually having to deal with the extra equipment necessary to move all that weight.

Meanwhile, ships stationed out near the asteroid belt, as well as satellites past Pluto's orbit kept a watchful eye on deep space for any sign of an oncoming fleet of enemy vessels.

Aboard the command deck of the Cagliostro, Mark Johnson stood staring at the view screen with his hands clasped behind his back, his mind deep in somber thought.

"Quarter for your thoughts, sugar?"

Mark turned towards the voice, and smiled at Ariel as she slipped in beside him and wrapped her arms around his waist. He in turn wrapped his around hers.

"Just wondering where they are, Ari, as usual," he added.

"You sound like you want them to come after us."

"No, don't be confused about that. I'd rather they turn around and run as far away from our quadrant of space as possible. But that's not going to happen. There's no doubt about it Ariel, they are coming for us. It's only a matter of when."

"You sound worried."

"I am Ari, I am. The Earth has what? Maybe a thousand ships between all the nations upon it? There may be ten times that number coming for us, for all that we know."

"Do you really believe that?" she asked in almost a whisper, as she turned and stared up at him.

"Of course I do. I'd rather be wrong and exaggerate something like the number of heavy ships we'll be facing then underestimate them. This is not a good situation. If they get to Earth, our ground forces worldwide should be able to handle them if we can take out the majority of them up here. Unless they simply destroy the planet from space."

Ariel stared at him, wide eyed in disbelief, "Are you serious? You think they can crush the planet from orbit? I-I thought you weren't afraid of their weapons? You said ours were better, didn't you?"

"From what we saw on our journey across the stars, yes, I believe our weaponry is more advanced."

"Then why are you saying they could destroy the planet from space? We can't do that."

"Actually Ari, we could. Very easily too. A nuke attached to a quantum singularity generator fired into a planet. The nuke explodes and crushes the planets crust as the singularity generator is triggered upon impact and instantly the planet becomes a black hole and sucks in upon itself. It's the cosmic death of a world in under two minutes flat."

"You can do that?" she asked incredulously.

He shrugged, "I've theoretically been able to do that for the past ten years, actually. It's a doomsday measure, something I'll never use, unless the Earth is destroyed. Then I will fly to the home world of who and whatever has done this to us and send every last one of them to hell." He stared her in the face as he finished his last sentence.

"I had no idea you had worked that all out," she murmured.

"It's not something I talk about. President Scaleia knows I can make it happen. He's the only person as far as I know."

"B-but you would have to manufacture everything you need to do this, right? It would take a long time to create, right?" Ariel asked with a growing fear in the pit of her stomach.

"Read my mind Ari, you tell me."

She looked into his mind and her face went taut with fear. "My God, y-you have everything you need to do this, to destroy a world, right onboard this ship," she stammered out, in shock.

He nodded stoically.

"I have that and a lot more as well, Ari. These people are coming here for a fight, you heard that alien bastard who was torturing us. This is no joke. They wanted to destroy us before we reached the stars. Now we have. How many of our space ships over the years have they blown up? Does it go back to the 1970's and the Apollo missions? Or the 1980's and 2000's when our shuttles were destroyed? These aliens have been trying to dissuade us from coming to space for years. How many of our people have they killed? Hell, how many have they kidnapped, and replaced with clones or shape shifters? We'll never know."

"But Mark, you'd kill an entire world?"

"If they destroyed our world? Yes, I would, in a heartbeat and with no regrets. I'd go to their home world and loose the world buster right down their throats."

"And what then? Where would we go after that happened?"

"Would it matter what we did at that point?"

"Everything matters!" Ariel bellowed.

"Only if we're alive, does it matter Ariel, and right now I'm trying to defend our world. I promise you I have no intention of using that weapon, ever, unless as a last resort for our survival or if our world is already destroyed. It is the ultimate final option. While I have no want or desire to use the world buster against any world, or people, it is always on the table."

"B-but Mark, an entire race! Their children…"

"Is it any less than they would do to us? My God Ari, I have parents that are still alive, as do you, as well as your brothers and sister. What about them? You'd let them just die unavenged?"

"I-I don't know."

"What about your sister Cherie's kids? These bastards mean to kill them as well as everyone else on this planet, because we supposedly frighten them, yet we have done nothing, let me repeat that, nothing, to any of these people.

They came to us and attacked, they kidnapped the General, then the President, then they tortured you and me and our entire crew. They killed forty of our people. This is no game. If they fear us, so be it, we'll show them what fear really is. I don't need to use the world buster, I have other weapons that will leave lasting impressions on them as well as any allies they may have. It's time for them to reap what they have sowed."

She sighed then, and shook her head plaintively, before looking up at Mark again, "Don't hurt innocents in this war Mark, whatever you do, please."

"Ariel, I am praying that none of this will come to pass, I am going to do everything I can to stop this, all of this, in its tracks. I don't want there to be a war with the first alien races we've ever met, I'd rather be going out there meeting them with the open hand of friendship, not the clenched fist of destruction. But the problem is Ari; I may not have a choice. If they come after us, like I'm sure they will, I will respond with everything I can come up with."

"What if you're wrong?"

"About what Ari?"

"About these aliens. What if they are more advanced than we are in everything they do? Spaceflight, weaponry, everything? What then?"

"Ari, what do you want me to do? Tell the President the Earth should just surrender to these things? They are more than willing to kill us all, without a second thought. This is the bottom of the ninth with two men out; this is all or nothing for the win, Ari. Seriously I understand your reservations, but as a planet we cannot lie down and just say, 'Do with us as you will. We mean you no harm.' That's just foolishness."

"You're right," she whispered as she leaned over and hugged him. He returned the embrace as they stared out the view screen.

The communicator system beeped and Ariel disengaged herself from Mark. She walked over to her desk, touching a control button and instantly Dan Sledge's voice reverberated across the command deck, "Mark, it's done. Everything should be one hundred percent operational now."

"All right Danny, thanks. I'm glad to hear it. Another ace up our sleeves. Join us on the command deck when you're ready."

"I'm on my way boss." Dan replied.

"What was that about?" Ari asked in wonder.

"Something I added to the Cagliostro as a 'just in case' measure."

"Not another something to destroy a world, I hope."

"Ariel, stop right there. That conversation is over."

"I know," she answered almost fearfully, but with trepidation at the very least.

The doors of the maglovator opened and Red, Eddie and Dan walked in looking grim.

"Everything okay with you three?"

"See for yourself, Boss." Red replied as he sat down behind his console and punched a button, revealing a new image across the command deck viewer. Mark's breath caught as he looked in wonder at what was displayed before him. Ariel slid up next to him nervously and gripped his hand.

"It's really the end of the world, isn't it?" she asked in a hushed breath.

"Not if I can help it," Mark replied grimly with a steadfast resolve that snapped them all out of their momentary fear.

"That's a lot of ships," Red offered.

"It doesn't matter, no matter what it takes, we're going to win this war and protect our world."

They all continued to stare as the sub-space feed they were viewing from a satellite out near Pluto showed thousands of ships, all large and heavily armed heading toward Earth. Then when most had passed the small world on the solar systems fringe, a burst of energy flared from one of the ships directed at the satellite they were viewing through, and almost instantly the view screen went decidedly dead.

Chapter Twenty Six

"Battle stations!" Mark shouted, as he punched a button on his virtual console, immediately causing a klaxon to sound across the ship.

Throughout the Cagliostro, people scurried and ran to places they needed to be. No one was off duty now. The entire ship was moving and alive.

Mark pointed to Ariel who immediately put him through to the ships interior communication system.

"This is Mark Johnson," he began, "I don't have to tell any of you what we're up against here, you already know. We're fighting for our survival, and judging by what was just detected coming for us, it's a vastly superior force. There may be five times as many ships in that fleet as we have. But we have a few surprises on our side. I'm hoping; no make that praying, they are enough. I suggest you pray as well. We all may be needing it today." He pointed at Ariel and the system shut down.

"All right Ari, put me through to General Abruzzi's ship."

"Okay Mark you're on," she nodded in reply.

"General," Mark began.

"Captain Johnson. How goes it aboard the Cagliostro?"

"We're as prepared as we're going to be, General."

"As we are across the rest of the fleet, Captain."

"Has the plan I suggested proven satisfactory?"

"Yes Captain, it has. The fleet is moving into position, or I should say positions as we speak. Let's just pray this all works."

"I'm ahead of you there sir." Mark replied stoically.

"Very good Johnson, let's move out then, shall we? The asteroid belt awaits. Fall in behind the 'Titan' until we get to position."

"We're on your four O'Clock, sir." Mark answered and then the comm went silent as first the war ship 'Titan', Abruzzi's ship, powered up its just installed magno-disc engines and disappeared in a burst of light followed closely by the Cagliostro and then nearly two hundred other ships blinked away behind them in elongated flashes of light.

Five minutes later, approximately two hundred ships of war exited hyper-warp and spread out amongst the three hundred that were already there.

"Lots of ships here, Mark," Red commented.

"These ships don't have hyper-warp tech, Red." Mark replied, "They began moving here before we left for that little dirt world Duddas, where we picked the real General up."

"Why? How'd anyone know to position 'em here?" Dan asked in surprise.

"The president and I worked that out before we left. Even while those ships were chasing us, this group was heading here, to lie in wait."

"So they were that group we made that end run through on our way back to earth?"

"Some of them were. Others were on their way." Mark shrugged as he answered in reply.

"This is gettin' better an' better." Dan shook his head in disbelief.

"Relax big guy, we need to be totally focused on this."

"I am boss, count on that."

"Always have, Danny."

"Gentlemen, we are here and moving into position." General Abruzzi's voice announced over the ships comm.

"God speed, General," Mark offered.

"And to you as well…Captain Johnson."

Mark smiled at this. But that did not change the butterflies in his stomach as he watched two disparate images on their view screen. One showed the ships of Earth lining up approximately a mile apart behind the asteroid field. The other was one beamed to everyone from deep space surveillance satellites between Jupiter and the asteroid field.

It showed ships streaking towards Earth, leaping into hyper-warp once more as they crossed into the solar system. A veritable herd of ships, filling the space before the camera on the satellite with their immense numbers.

"This isn't lookin' too cool," Eddie DiGenovese spoke aloud.

"Stay frosty, soldier." Mark replied.

"Hey boss, I stopped bein' a soldier years ago," the black haired man replied, "I liked bein' one then, and I liked doing my job."

"You were good at it DiGenovese, that's why I hired you. It sure as hell wasn't for your personality." Mark smirked.

"They're starting to spread out," Red announced.

"Visual." Mark commanded. Instantly the view screen image changed and one of the satellites on the other side of the asteroid field broadcast its feed directly to the Cag as well as every other ship in the fleet.

"Ariel, get the General back on the horn please."

"Aye, aye sir." She replied while adding a mocking salute to her response.

"I see somebody got over her nervousness."

She sighed, "Looks can be deceiving."

"Don't worry honey; I'm as nervous as the next guy."

"How come you ain't showin' it?" Dan asked.

"You know me Danny, on the outside cool as a cucumber. On the inside, well a little less cool."

"Just not by much," Eddie quipped, and everyone had a laugh. It was a laugh filled with anxiety, but a laugh nonetheless.

Ariel raised her hand and stopped everyone then. She turned toward Mark as she began to speak again, "I'm receiving a signal from...them," she stated enigmatically.

"Video or just audio?"

"Video, Mark."

"Let's see it."

The screen blinked before them and suddenly there was a yellow skinned alien with dark black eyes seated in a captain's chair aboard the bridge of a very militaristic looking ship. It was not bright and gleaming like the Cagliostro's command deck. It was dark with deep blues, blacks and maroons overrun with cables and wires running everywhere in sight. The yellow skinned aliens wide set, jet black eyes stared straight ahead with his hands clasped before him almost regally, as if he thought very highly of himself. He had a flat face, his nose was virtually non-existent. He appeared relaxed. He had no hair present anywhere on his skull. Not his face, nor his head. He looked straight into the camera and began to speak.

"People of Earth. Surrender your world and your lives to the Agalum. We have come for you. You have been judged and found wanting. We are the fist of the Agalum and have been sent to claim your lives and world. Surrender peacefully, and you will be treated fairly. Resist, and we will obliterate you."

Immediately in reply the Cagliostro's view screen split in two as General Abruzzi was now seen sitting aboard the Titan's command deck. Abruzzi snarled his reply, "If you want this world and its inhabitants you better prepare yourselves for a long, drawn out conflict, mister. If you know anything about us you know we don't give up without a fight, and isn't that what has you all afraid of us to begin with? Our ability to fight? You should turn around right now and head back to whatever swamp you crawled out of, son. I guarantee you'll wish you had when this is all over, if you survive at all."

The alien smirked, showing rows of glistening yellow teeth, "Ah, General Abruzzi, I had heard you were a tough man from your inquisitors. No matter though, when this is over you will kneel at my feet and beg for death."

Abruzzi squinted his eyes as he stared at the alien on the screen across from him, letting the air hang silent and dead for a long moment before he replied, "Try your damnedest, alien. I'm going to show you the error of everything your people did to me and my world the past

God only knows how many years. As my grandfather used to say, you pompous jackass, bring it!"

Abruzzi immediately had the connection cut, leaving the alien to fill the Cagliostro's screen fully. Mark motioned to Ariel and she cut their view of the alien ships bridge as well.

"Did you see the bridge on that thing? It looked like it was held together with bailing wire an' bubble gum," Danny commented.

"Don't underestimate them, any of you. We really have no idea what we're up against. For all we know, they could obliterate us instantly," Mark admonished.

"Hey Mr. Cheery, give it a rest for now, we ain't beaten yet," Dan replied.

"The Titan is moving," Red advised.

Abruzzi's ship placed itself before all the rest, on the Earth side of the asteroid belt.

"Agalum." Mark murmured.

"What Mark?" Eddie asked.

"He said they were called the 'Agalum' what does that mean? Who was called that? His race in particular? Or the entirety of all the races involved in this little group of thugs? Or maybe the race that runs the whole show?"

"We'll have to ask them after we kick their asses," Ariel offered with a grin.

"After we kick their asses Ari, you can be the first to ask that question of every one of them, just do it as painfully as possible. We owe them that much."

She nodded with a smile, and turned back to her control console.

"Dan, bring us into position."

"Will do, boss." the big navigator and pilot answered.

"Battle stations people, this time it's for real," Mark announced, leaning forward in his seat.

The 'Cagliostro' swept to the right of the 'Titan' spreading about two miles between them before coming to a halt and holding position. Other ships in the fleet did likewise, following down the line in either direction on the earth-side of the asteroid belt.

"Now what?" Red asked.

"Now the fun begins," Mark replied as he nodded to Ari, who immediately queued up the comm system, leading to the General's face appearing on the main viewer.

"We're ready, General."

"Okay Johnson, let's get this show on the road, then."

Across the depths of space the two fleets stared at each other, the earth fleet was made up of men who were walking a razor's edge of fear and trepidation, but the alien fleet? Who knew? They were an unknown quantity. Were they as afraid as the humans fighting for their own lives? Or were they simply emotionless killers carrying out their orders? No one knew. Not Mark Johnson, not General Abruzzi.

Suddenly the Titan coughed a burst of energy from its forward most guns that streaked across space, between free-floating asteroids and exploded against the hull of the alien command ship. The blast was potent; it shifted the Agalum war ship in space, actually moving it from the impact, knocking it aside as if it was in slow motion. But by that time all the ships on either side of it began firing, sending blasts through the asteroid field at their enemies. Space was lit up like a city at night with flashes of light and the corresponding explosions. The breadth and scope of it all was intimidating. For the first time in human history, the people of Earth were at war with someone other than themselves.

"Shields holding up okay?" Mark asked as the ship rocked seemingly to the sound of thunder as each blast it received was felt throughout its stout hull.

"Yeah, all good so far," Red replied.

"Eddie, try to actually hit something," Mark jibed his weapons officer.

"I've hit everythin' I shot at boss." The marksman replied through gritted teeth. His HUD holding steadily before his eyes as he fired again and again.

"That's one hell of a lot of ships," Red remarked quietly.

"No kidding," Mark replied stoically. "Time for phase two."

He pointed again at Ari, who immediately opened a channel to the Titan, "General phase two is a go, sir?"

"That it is Mr. Johnson that it is. Initiating phase two on my command...Initiate!" The elder warrior announced authoritatively as the earth ships began to back away from the asteroid belt while firing. Instantly the alien marauders followed them into the belt itself.

"How are we doing?" Mark asked Red.

"We've lost two ships so far, and twenty two others are damaged appreciably. On their side we've taken out about forty of their ships. But there are so damned many of them, by my calculations they will overrun and overwhelm us."

Mark grinned wolfishly, "Not by mine, Red."

Mark stabbed at a button on his virtual console and the asteroid belt lit up with a blinding flash of light so bright everyone covered their eyes just before the view screen automatically dimmed to filter out the harsh light.

"What the hell?" Eddie asked in surprise.

"Eddie shut up and lock and load. Full attack on anything that comes through that hell!"

Dan turned back and looked at Mark smiling, "You sly fox, you mined the asteroid belt."

"Bingo Mr. Sledge." Mark replied with a slight grin.

***

All throughout the asteroid belt, explosions reverberated as asteroids from the size of pebbles to the size of whole states collided with the enemy vessels with catastrophic results. Explosions, silent but for the lack of oxygen to carry that sound, lit the star scape brightly. Ships were crushed, sending plumes of ionized debris upward, downward and to both sides of every ship that was caught between the massive asteroids in horrific collisions.

Asteroids and ships rebounded chaotically, lighting up the Cagliostro's sensor board and view screen as the great ship split off from the Titan and began to cut to the right, away from the much larger war ship, attacking anything that was getting through. Several ships of the Earth fleet followed the Cag, strafing enemy vessels that the Cag had already passed.

But it was not going to be enough.

"Mark!" Shouted Red Robinski, "Too many are getting through the line!"

Just then the General's visage filled the view screen, behind him the command deck of his ship was in pandemonium. Lights flashed and klaxon's sounded as people were seen running to and fro. The image blurred several times while explosions sounded through the speakers.

"Johnson! We're going to meet their flagship head on. If I don't make it, the 'Titan' I mean, you have command of the fleet. You've served us all well so far and everyone here owes you a debt of gratitude we can never repay. They will listen and more importantly advise you as well."

"General, stop it!" Mark commanded, "The Titan is damaged, you've taken a lot of hits and that flagship has been hiding behind other vessels, biding its time. It's unscathed. You might as well be starting a suicide mission. Wait for us to get to you; we'll fight our way through together. The Cagliostro is barely scratched. Don't be foolish; don't sacrifice yourself and your crew."

Abruzzi looked at him stoically before replying, "That's what I always liked about you Johnson, you always speak your mind. No, son, I'm not going to wait. I have to hold that ship back from breaking our line no matter what the cost. We're spread out right now over a hundred thousand miles from each other. That's too short a distance for you to hyper-warp to my aid, and at regular speeds it will take you too long to get here before I have to engage that ship. But I have to stop them from getting any further. Your asteroid mining was a good idea and tactic, but there are far too many of these bastards left out here and that big ship of theirs is not going to get any closer to Earth while I can help it."

"We're on our way, General." Mark replied, grim faced.

"God Speed, Johnson," the General replied.

"The same to you sir," Mark answered, his expression pained.

The view screen returned to a view of space. Explosions continued to flare across the panorama of the image before their eyes—bursts of light flaring to brightness and then fading away.

"Full ahead on the Titan's position," Mark ordered.

"Aye, aye sir," Dan replied.

"Mr. Di Genovese, I'm sure I don't have to tell you to shoot anything that gets in our way, and blow it straight to hell, do I?"

"Not at all, sir." Eddie replied, as he began firing the ships massive solar cannons at full strength.

Almost instantly the Cagliostro was under fire from several fronts at once, energy flaring across her shields, which glowed brighter with every hit.

The Cagliostro cut a line though the enemy ships, darting on end under Dan's steady hands while its cannons exploded with fury, smashing enemy ships with solar blast after solar blast.

"Incoming!" Red shouted, as he diverted power to certain shield generators manually. The ship rumbled as twin missiles fired from the invaders before them exploded harmlessly on the Cagliostro's next generation shields.

"How are the shields holding up?"

"Better than the ones we replaced, that's for sure. She's taking a pounding, but they're hardly losing strength. They're down to ninety-four percent right now. We're doing well so far," Red replied.

"Good, how's the Titan?"

"She's under siege. Surrounded and alone out there, we're the closest ship to her and she's still two minutes away."

"Just get us there," Mark answered quietly, resting his chin on his clenched fist, staring straight ahead at the view screen. "Hang on General," he muttered as he stared straight ahead. Ariel turned her head to look at him, pain reflected in her own eyes, and then returned her gaze to the control panel before her.

"We're thirty seconds out, Mark," Dan announced.

"DiGenovese, fire on anything that's even remotely near the Titan, starting now."

"We're still twenty seconds out of range yet."

"Just do it!" Mark ordered angrily as the Cagliostro's cannons began to fire again. Strafing everything before them further away than the naked eye could see. The seconds each seemed like an eternity as the Cagliostro drew closer to the beleaguered Titan.

Suddenly a bright explosion filled space as the Cagliostro hurtled onwards, instantly the screen dimmed to compensate, but everyone knew what they had just seen without it being verbalized.

Ariel continued to speak into her headset, almost pleading for a reply, but none was forthcoming. Finally Red turned back towards Mark, "The Titan. Mark, she's…gone."

Chapter Twenty Seven

Mark stared at the view screen as specks of steel burned away from the explosion that had consumed the Titan. Flecks of burning debris shone brightly as they arced away from the war ships death, finally burning off and disappearing into the depths of space.

Four ships had surrounded the Titan and had brought a devastating attack upon her. She gave a good accounting of herself as two of the ships now billowed smoke into space. Each was a mile long behemoth, and each of those two was in bad shape.

The other two ships were another story. They were barely scratched. One of those two was the command ship.

The four ships turned in space, seemingly almost in slow motion as they came about to face the Cagliostro. Then they spread out from one another, creating a greater distance between themselves. Nearby, other ships in their fleet positioned themselves equidistantly as well.

"What are they doing?" Ariel asked quietly.

"Boss, I don't like this at all," Red announced.

"Agreed. Full reverse. Tell the other ships to reverse as well, reconnoiter back on the other side of the asteroid field.

Suddenly the ship at the furthest end of the line opposing the Cagliostro and the remaining Earth ships began to glow from two protruding rods that had emerged from the bow of each of the alien ships. Energy crackled like lightning in space first across the two prongs on the ship at the far end of the group, and then it leaped to the next one, and then the next and then the one after that. In less time than it would take to tell it, ever one of the enemy ships was connected to that almost living arc of energy thousands of miles wide across space.

"Full reverse and all power to forward shields; steal it from life support if you have to. Front shields need to be powered up more than any other system on these ships now, and keep reversing."

"Boss! What are you doing?" Eddie asked, wide-eyed.

"Trying to save all our lives," Johnson barked in reply.

Instantly the arc sprang forward, leaping from the prows of all the enemy ships positioned across the gulf of space from their Earth-born foes, simultaneously.

The arc of energy slammed into the asteroid field, disintegrating everything before it, shattering asteroids, and detonating un-exploded mines, burning the depths of space white hot before the Cagliostro's crew's stunned eyes.

Several slower moving Earth ships were caught in the wave of energy. The arc tore through them like they had no shielding at all, decimating the ships of the fleet and leaving them either de-powered or simply decimated.

The Cag backed away quickly, followed closely by less than a hundred other remaining ships.

Johnson stood as he watched the arc slowly gaining on them as they backed away, covering thousands of miles in instants.

"Prepare to go to hyper-warp," Dan advised.

"No, wait," Mark ordered. "That arc or wave or whatever you want to call it is losing cohesiveness."

"He's right," Red replied, "it's falling apart somehow, it must be reaching the end of its limits of travel," he apprised as he watched his sensor grid. "What's left of it is still going to impact us, brace yourselves, 'cause here it comes."

Almost as soon as Red had advised it, the Cagliostro was buffeted horribly, violently slammed as if by a gargantuan fist in space, the ship spun across the void out of control. Sparks flew from control panels across the command deck, and then everything went dark as the Cagliostro lay horribly askew in space, seemingly teetering helplessly on end.

Nearby, the much larger ships that had survived the battle and had been gathering with the Cag were also similarly devastated by the attack. Smoke and sparks curled into the airless void. The Earth fleet floated, decimated in space and powerless.

"What was that? What the hell did they hit us with?" Dan asked, in stunned shock.

"Some variation of that energy sucking attack they used on us in deep space," Mark replied as he rubbed his head. "Is everyone okay?"

Ariel, Red, Dan and Eddie all replied affirmatively.

"Do we have any power left?"

"Emergency only Mark, not enough to start the magno-discs," Dan answered.

"What about the rest of the fleet? Are any other ships viable?" Mark asked desperately.

Ariel merely shook her head, fear playing across her eyes as she did.

"Find me power, we have to start the engines."

"Wait Mark, look!" Red pointed at the view screen as over a thousand of the massive enemy ships began to pass them, heading towards Earth.

"Th-they're ignoring us." Eddie announced, wide eyed in surprise.

"We're beneath them now. We can't fight back, or they think we're all dead already. Either way it's their mistake," Mark growled menacingly.

He sprang from his seat, "Danny you're with me, I think I have an idea, but we have to hurry."

"Okay Mark, let's go." The big native of Jupiter's moons stood and answered as he followed Mark into the maglovator.

Once inside, Dan turned towards Mark and asked, "So what's the plan?"

Johnson shrugged, and answered in a low voice, "I don't have one. I'm fresh out."

Dan looked at him wide eyed and incredulous, "Are you kiddin' me? Now's not the time fer foolin' around Mark. The whole damned planet needs you. You gotta have somethin' up your sleeve?"

Mark looked up at his friend, "I'm trying to work it out Danny, but I can't. They steamrolled us. What'd I miss? There has to be something."

"No, we didn't miss anythin'. They had numbers on us, by a freakin' big margin too. But now ain't the time to be thinkin' about that. C'mon Mark, you're the only guy I know smarter 'n me. Let's get this baby fired up again and get after those creeps."

"Danny, I should have hyper-warped us out of there, we'd still be in the fight right now."

"It wouldn't matter, Mark. We're out gunned an' outnumbered. We need a big thing, like what they used against us. Somethin' ta even the odds. Usin' the asteroid belt was a good start, but we needed more'n that."

"I know," was Mark's terse reply. He touched the cuff of his sleeve and spoke, "Ariel, any word from Earth yet?"

"No Mark, not yet."

"What about the other ships damaged in the attack? Are any of them under power again?"

"No Mark, I have no contact with any other ship that was hit by that dampening wave."

"I guess that's as good a name as any for that damned weapon," he replied, talking more to Dan then to Ariel. "Ariel the first that you hear of anything let me know. We're going to try to kick start the engines, somehow. Johnson out." He clicked his right sleeve once more, silencing the communicator.

"If those ships ain't near Earth yet they can't be usin' hyper-warp."

"They could but at a much lower speed. At one quarter light speed it will take them about 17 minutes."

Ariel's voice interrupted them both, "Mark I've been monitoring your conversation. According to Red, those ships won't reach Earth for about two hours at the speed they are currently traveling at."

"Thanks Ari. We'll be back up there soon." He nodded, looking at Dan then added, "That's one of the first things that's gone our way since all this madness started."

"Yeah, you got that right. So what are you thinking? Usin' the 'Grazer and the shuttles again to kick start the Cag?"

"I wish it were that easy, Dan, but they were hit by the same dampening technology that hit the Cag itself this time."

"So what're you thinkin'?"

"Something drastic," he smiled menacingly at Dan.

"Okay now you got me scared. What, nuclear?"

"Yes. Setting off one of the nukes I had loaded aboard before we headed out on this mission."

"I didn't know you had nukes added."

"That's right, no one did. Abruzzi and the President thought that every ship should have nukes aboard in case we had to use them as a last line of defense against these marauders. Now we don't even have the power to fire one at any of those ships."

"Maybe the ship don't..." Dan smiled then. It was not one of his pleasant, almost happy go-lucky grins, it was menacing.

The two men entered the armory and both put on the armored battle suits the crew had used earlier to board the space station several weeks back. As the clear blue tinted visors slid into place, the suits sealed with a hiss.

Dan's suit was bulky and large, covering his massive body tightly, mimicking his powerful muscles beneath its armored surface. Mark's was sleeker and tighter fitting. Both were based on the ships skin technology adding armored resistance to energy shields.

"These things have power, huh?" Dan asked, his voice modulated through the communicator built into the armored suit.

"Yes, like the sensitive ships systems, such as life support and communications, I was able to shield them from the majority of the dampening wave's effect. Hell, if their dampening power was the same as we had originally faced weeks back, we'd have been fine. But the way they amplified it through most of their fleet…" his voice trailed off.

"What?" Danny asked.

"Maybe nothing, but I think I have an idea."

"You gonna clue me in?"

"Would you say that at least most of those ships are linked together somehow to be able to produce that energy wave?"

"Yes, of course. There'd have ta be some kinda link between the ones engaged in that attack, at least."

"Good, let's go to the heavy ordinance wing, and then you're going to have to carry something very heavy."

"A nuke, you want me ta carry a nuke."

"I always said you were the smartest guy I knew, besides me at least." Mark grinned as he exited the armory with Dan following.

Crewmen hustled about the corridors of the Cagliostro now as the two armor suited men drew closer to the heavy ordinance wing. Most crewmen didn't even give Mark or Dan a second look as they scrambled, trying to get sensitive systems back online.

Mark tapped the door control on the wall, but nothing happened. He looked overhead and saw only emergency lighting on.

"Blast, its dead down here. Dan, I need you." He pointed at the doors, then he spoke over his suits speaker system, "Everyone on this deck clear out immediately, I need this deck empty of all personnel besides Dan Sledge and myself."

Immediately without hesitation all the crewmembers on that level headed to the maglovators and filed out.

Mark turned back to Dan, "Ready?"

Sledge nodded and forced his fingers into the seam between the doors; bending omnium steel like it was paper. Then with a slight pull, he forced the doors apart. Mark nodded approvingly as they entered the heavy ordinance bay.

"Here." Mark pointed. In the corner were several magnetically sealed and isolated containers.

"Nukes," Sledge commented.

"Yes, all ready to be mounted on a missile and fired. Only this time this one is going to be thrown."

"By me. I get it."

"I know you do. C'mon, time is running out on us and the Earth."

He tapped his sleeve once again, "Ariel, any word from any one yet?"

Her voice crackled weakly and static filled over his headset, "None yet. We're too deep in space and being almost powerless we can't access subspace communications."

Mark shook his head and pursed his lips in disgust, "I'm about to rectify that problem… at least I hope I am."

Then he cut the communications link. Mark turned toward Dan, "Are you ready Danny?"

The big man nodded in his armored suit, the blue visored faceplate moving up and down. "Which one you want me to grab?"

"The one closest to you. Then let's move."

They exited the heavy ordinance bay, Dan carrying a forty-ton nuke in front of him as they walked precariously down the hall towards the shuttle and landing bay.

"Are you okay?" Mark asked.

"Yeah, yeah, I'm fine. This thing's heavy, but I'm strong enough to handle it."

"I know, that's one of the reasons why I rely on you."

"When this is over I want a raise, ya know."

Mark laughed for a half second, then moved to open the landing bay inner access doors. He hit a sequence of numbers and the doors slid slowly open.

"Hhhmm, there's some power left down here yet, just enough to open the doors it seems."

"I guess all your shielding did manage to protect a few systems, at least a little bit," Dan replied.

"It was better than nothing, I guess," Mark answered.

The two men walked into the big hanger deck, Dan balancing and carrying the forty-ton warhead like it was a garbage can held out before him.

"So what am I doin' with this thing?" Dan inquired.

"Do you see that powerless and derelict Agalum ship out there? It's probably only about a mile or two from us?"

"Uhh, yeah. What about it?" Dan answered pensively.

"Throw that war head at it. When it makes contact I'm going to blow it remotely."

"Uhhh, are you thinkin' this through?" Dean asked incredulously, "That's seriously a mile out there. I don't know if I can hit that from here. That thing is maybe as big as the Cag; it's not one of the mile long ships. Chances are I'm gonna miss it."

Mark smiled, "No you won't, Danny. I have complete faith in you."

"Yeah? Well that's more'n I got right about now, boss-man."

"Look Dan, once you get it clear of the ship, inertia and weightlessness will do the rest. Just throw it out there when I tell you. In fact you can put it down right there for now and give me a hand over here."

Dan lowered it with a suppressed thud as it hit the deck. Then he walked over to where Mark was standing, as Mark began to open a crate that was stored near the doors.

"What's this?" Dan asked curiously.

"Something I put together immediately after we returned. When I saw what our enemy could do with their dampening technology. It's an induction unit. Made to absorb heat and radiation and convert it to energy to turn the magno-discs over in case something like this happened again. But I never thought about using a nuke to jump start it. It was all going to be solar based. Unfortunately, it will take hours to absorb that much solar energy. Earth will be a stinking crater by then."

"It may be anyway by the time we get back there," Dan added stoically.

"No," Mark turned and shouted at his friend. "I will not give up, not now, not ever. We will beat them back there and then I'll do whatever it takes to send them back to their own worlds, or straight to hell, whichever comes first!"

Dan put his hands up in mock defense. "All right buddy, I'm with you to the very end. You know that already. Just tell me what to do."

"Throw these two panels out towards that derelict ship. They don't have to get that far away, just as long as they are facing that ship. The heavy leads from each will hook to this device which is connected to the starting cells on each magno-disc engine. I'm going to open the landing bay doors now. We're going to lose oxygen, and this section will decompress. Best to magnetize your boots to the floor."

"What about the shuttles and the 'Grazer?"

"Maintenance crews secured them before we engaged the enemy. They'll be fine."

The bay doors opened and the oxygen within the landing bay whooshed out explosively, both men held onto handles built into the solid steel walls until the pressure equalized within the landing bay.

Dan then took the two ten foot long panels of glistening white material and heaved one after the other towards the unmoving Agalum ship, which besides an occasional spark or errant plume of smoke from something within burning up, was seemingly quite dead.

Mark attached the leads from each panel to the control interface he was standing in front of. "We're ready Danny. Heave the nuke as far as you can. Try to hit that damned ship out there. We need the mass from it to make this work."

"I'll do my best, boss."

"Your best is hitting it, Dan."

The big man looked at Mark and nodded, then waved his hand for Mark to stand clear. Lifting the forty-ton warhead up once more, he began to swing it like a shot putter, around and around, never taking his eyes off his target, then once he built up considerable speed, he let it go, directly at his target. The bomb hurtled through space, aimed unerringly at the unmoving vessel.

Mark shut the bay doors and oxygen once again flooded the landing bay. On the monitor for his console, he watched as the nuke slammed into the floating ship. He punched a button with the bottom of his fist, and the screen they were watching went blazingly white. Their visors on the armored suits they both wore turned black instantly as the monitor itself turned jet black automatically as well.

Immediately the great ship rumbled as it sprang to life about them. The magno-disc engines began to whir, slowly at first, then building power mightily. All about the ship systems blazed back to life.

Ariel's voice shouted from the communicators within each man's suit, "We're back to full power."

"Hyper-warp now!" Mark roared.

The Cagliostro leaped towards Earth, disappearing in a blaze of distorted starlight.

Thirty seconds later it exited hyper-warp as both men still wearing their armored suits entered the command deck. Immediately two awaiting techs helped them out of their bulky armored suits. A pilot named Edmundson stood as Dan approached the pilot's chair and stepped aside without a word letting Dan slide back behind his control panel.

Mark cursed loudly as the view came into focus. Earth was being bombarded from space by well over a thousand vessels, as the outnumbered Earth ships who were still trying to blockade the planet fought bravely against their enemies.

Chapter Twenty Eight

Mark Johnson stood up from his command chair and walked towards the main viewer, his mouth hung open slightly for an instant, in shock. The scene before them stunned everyone on the command deck to silence. Space above Earth was lit up with energy blasts and explosions as well as missile contrails striking from Earth.

Massive space stations in Earth's orbit fired blasts of golden energy at the attacking ships, as hundreds of one-man attack vessels poured from the orbiting stations as well as from the planet's surface.

The enemy assault ships fired powerful energy blasts, disintegrating the small one-man ships instantly, as they in turn were blasted by the next wave of small attack craft. Mile long 'Dreadnaught' class Earth ships formed blockades about the space stations, using their own mass to protect the vulnerable orbiting city-sized space stations. Powerful deck cannons fired missiles and energy upon the enemy ships, decimating them.

But it was slowly, once again, becoming a matter of numbers. It was now the denizens of one planet against the soldiers of many. Even with the massive planet-wide retaliation, the surface of the Earth was in turmoil. Streamers of enemy fire raked the planet below, leaving a scorched Earth in its wake.

"Mark!" Ariel began with stunned trepidation edging her voice, "Cities are burning. New York, Chicago,

London, Tokyo, Los Angeles, they're all in flames, and more are being attacked at every moment."

"This is like the end of the world," Dan murmured.

"It will be Dan, unless we do something about it. There has to be a way to stop this." Mark's jaw set grimly in determined fury.

Red turned to him, "Cut the head off and the tail dies."

"What?" Mark snapped, turning towards his tactical officer.

"The command ship. We take that down; this all goes to hell. Well, hopefully at least." He shrugged.

"And what if it doesn't? It's a good start and I'm not discounting it, but we need to destroy this fleet completely."

Red cocked his head sideways before continuing, "Start with the command ship, it's as good a place as any. The rest we can make up as we go."

Mark nodded in agreement, "All right, let's do that."

"Mark, what about that dampening weapon of theirs? You know they're going to use it again and drain all these ships and stations of power?" Dan offered.

"Yeah, I do Danny, I'm working on that right now, I have a few ideas and you and I are going to talk about that after we take out that command ship." Johnson turned back to Red, "Where is that damned ship?"

"Trying to find her now, boss. There's lots of static out here, blocking sensors. They're trying to hide it."

"Where's the static thickest? The most concentrated?"

"Ummm, this makes no sense," Ariel exclaimed.

"What is it Ari?" Mark snapped.

She turned to look at him, "The largest concentration of what we're referring to as 'static' is coming from Mars. Actually, behind it."

"Sonuva-" Mark trailed off. "They're hiding the command vessel behind the red planet. That's why they cleared us from the asteroid belt. Whoever's in command of this attack is orchestrating it from the dark side of Mars."

"The cowards!" Dan blurted out angrily. "They're usin' their troopers like cannon fodder. They don't care how many die, as long as the bosses are safe an' sound. Sittin' back sippin' their lattes."

"For all we know they may all be clones, which would make sense actually," Red offered.

"Ari contact command, tell them what we are doing and where we are going. Warn them about that energy dampening attack they used on us, send them all the pertinent information we gathered on that attack before everything went dark, then tell them I'm working on something to counter it, but first we're going to take out the command ship."

"Got it," she replied.

"Dan, get us back to Mars. Hyper-warp. Now!"

The Cagliostro exploded away from Earth as if it was shot out of a cannon, space blurred around it and the great manta-ray shaped ship disappeared, starlight reflecting off of its mirrored surface as it streaked away towards the red planet.

"Exit hyper-warp on the opposite side of the planet. Now it's time to try out some of those improvements we installed after our shakedown run, Dan."

Sledge nodded his big head grimly upon his muscular neck and shoulders, "Reflective skin?"

"Yes, I was saving it for something just like this situation."

"We're exiting hyper-warp now," Dan commented.

"Turn on the reflective skin as soon as we exit."

Dan nodded. "Done and done."

"Let's hope it works," Eddie added.

"Agreed," Mark replied

"Where to now, boss? Around the planet?"

"Yes, try to keep us close to the planet but stay out of the atmosphere; I don't want them to see any heat ripples from us skirting what little atmosphere there is. Red, the Mars stations have all been evacuated, correct?"

"Yeah, they did that days ago, actually when we returned everyone was recalled. All our people are out of there."

Mark nodded silently.

"What are you thinking boss?" Eddie asked.

"Don't worry about it DiGenovese. It's something nasty, and if I decide to do it you'll be the first to know."

Mark clenched his teeth and set his lip as thoughts and calculations flew through his mind quickly.

"Bring us about, Mr. Sledge. It's time to confront our enemy face to face."

The Cagliostro shimmered as the reflective skin took effect, more akin to a chameleon's ability more than to true invisibility. But still the ship seemed to disappear, its graceful shape blending in with the space about it as it sailed around the curvature of the red planet towards its opposite side.

"Uhhh, Mark," Red began, "the shields are down, you do know that right?"

"Can't be helped, Red. It's part of the reflective skin. For now we have to rely on our armored hull. Hopefully we won't need either armor or shields, for now."

"And that just make me feel all the more secure," Red replied hesitantly.

The Cagliostro silently flew to the side of Mars away from the Sun, and almost immediately Mark ordered, "Full stop."

Dan eased the throttle down on his virtual control panel as everyone upon the command deck caught their breath and stared silently at what was before them.

"I didn't realize that thing was so *big*," Eddie announced in an awed whisper.

"Yeah that's one word for it I guess," Dan replied, just as stunned by what he saw.

The ship that faced them was akin to a small city. It was tremendous, dwarfing the giant battleships that even now fought above the Earth.

"How come we didn't realize how large this thing was earlier?" Red asked.

"Too many other ships around it at the same time I suppose, plus we were in battle. Some of its mass had to be hidden. At least that's what I'm going with, for now." Mark replied.

"So what do we do now? This thing is so big it's ridiculous. I mean it's almost the size of Manhattan Island."

"I know Dan, I know. It's probably got ridiculous firepower as well." Mark paused a second before continuing, "But so do we."

"Ariel put me through to the heavy ordinance bay please."

She looked at him warily, narrowing her eyes to slits, and then she clicked a few buttons on her virtual control panel. "They're up, Mark."

"Gentlemen I need the Planet Buster weapon readied for immediate firing."

All heads on the deck turned to stare at Mark when he spoke.

"You're going to use it?"Ari asked incredulously.

"Yes I am. I don't care if I have to take Mars down to do it either. It's a lifeless rock, and Earth is all that matters right now. Everyone on the Earth is counting on us to save them, and we are about to."

Everyone on the command deck stared first at Ariel then at Mark, then back to Ariel once again.

Finally she spoke, "Mark, I'm not arguing with you on this. I'm not trying to be your conscience, not at all. I want this to work, if it's going to save our world."

"So do I Ariel, so do I. I don't just want this to work, I expect it to."

She nodded then, setting her beautiful jaw firmly, before answering, "Good, then let's blow these bastards straight to hell, where they belong."

"How are you gonna do this boss?" Dan asked, "You gonna fire it into the planet or directly at the ship?"

"Danny, I have to get through their shields first to nuke 'em outright, which with our nukes payloads shouldn't be a problem, it'll probably disintegrate that ship instantly, but I don't know that it will definitely. If I sacrifice Mars, its larger mass will cause them to be sucked in to the black hole or singularity that will exist there temporarily."

"What about us? We'll be sucked in too, won't we?"

"No, Eddie. If we hyper-warp the instant that missile is away, we'll be fine."

"I say open the singularity up in their faces. Use their ship for the mass." Everyone turned towards the sound of Ariel's voice. "What? It's the logical thing to do. Hit them straight on. After everything these bastards have done to us this past few weeks, they deserve to be nuked." Her voice was vehement as she finished.

Suddenly the Cagliostro rocked hard as a klaxon went off.

"We're under attack!" Red shouted.

"No, really?" Eddie replied.

"They saw through the reflective skin," Dan announced.

"Shields full strength, double front, damage control I need assessments yesterday," Mark commanded.

The Cagliostro began to weave through space, energy blasts sparking on its shields as the great ship swooped and dove to and fro majestically under Dan's deft manipulations.

"Heavy ordinance, what's your status?" Ariel shouted as the ship shook again from another hit.

"The weapon is being loaded now, command." A static filled voice replied frantically.

Again the ship rocked violently as Dan flipped it over and shot away from the planet at an angle. Dan's face was tense as sweat dripped down his brow, even though the command deck was cool, which he wiped with the back of his hand.

"How's our hull integrity?" Mark questioned, exuding calm and confidence even though it seemed like hell was exploding all about them.

"Hull integrity is strong but dropping steadily with each hit," Red replied, "Shields are taking a beating from that thing. We're down to fifty eight percent now."

"Just keep that ship within range, Danny. We're only going to get one shot at this."

"Understood, boss-man," Dan replied nervously as he fought the controls.

"Mark!" Ariel shouted, "We're being hailed by the enemy ship."

Mark looked at her sideways at first, and then nodded. Instantly the same yellow skinned alien with the large black eyes they had encountered earlier appeared on the view screen, "Greetings human Captain," the alien began. "You will immediately surrender your crew and your ship will, of course, be destroyed. That is the only 'deal' that will be put forth."

"Here's the only answer you're ever going to get, you mass murdering sonuvabitch! This one's for General Abruzzi!" Mark replied as he punched a glowing red button on his virtual control board.

Instantly the missile carrying the war head leaped from the underbelly of the manta-ray shaped vessel, streaking across space towards its intended prey. A heartbeat after the missile left its launch tube, the Cagliostro disappeared in a burst of light.

***

Aboard the Agalum command ship, the alien commander shouted, "Battle stations!" then continued with, "Shields at full! Brace for impact!" as the missile streaked unerringly towards the huge ship. "These foolish humans dare to fire a missile at our vessel? Surely they underestimate us."

"Commander!" one of his subordinates shouted in obvious fear, "That weapon is nuclear!"

"What?" The commander leapt from his seat and stared incredulously as the nuclear warhead exploded upon their shields, spreading light as great as a newborn star out behind Mars

***

A hundred thousand miles away the Cagliostro stood stationary and all aboard watched as the nuke exploded, sending cascading waves of radiation across the Agalum command ships shields, instantly collapsing them.

"Boom." The word escaped Mark's lips as he watched the second component of the planet buster begin to work. Built to destroy a world, the quantum singularity generator had no problem using the mass of the city-sized ship itself to create a smaller, but still powerful artificial black hole that sucked the Agalum vessel into its maw, crushing it like wadded paper.

The enemy command and control ship disappeared into the event horizon of the black hole, crushed to less than one tenth its size. After he watched it disappear, Mark touched another button on his console, which fired a second missile that streaked towards the artificial singularity and impacted upon its spinning maw, exploding just as brightly as the

264

first had, only this missile held a component that reversed the flow of the artificial singularities direction, effectively shutting it down.

Dan, Red and Eddie all turned and looked at him with their jaws dropped and their faces white.

"When'd you discover how to do that?" Eddie asked.

"A while ago, to be honest. Discovering how to shut it down was the hard part. It had to do with varying radioactive frequencies and such. It's all very complicated." He waved his hand dismissing it.

"Dan, get us back to Earth pronto," Mark ordered. "We have a war to finish and fires to put out."

The Cagliostro spun on its axis in space and disappeared into hyper-warp, leaving streaks of light behind it.

Seconds later it emerged above Earth, as battles raged all about space above the blue-green planet.

"Ariel, put me through on every damned frequency we have."

"All bands are activated," she acknowledged.

"Agalum vessels, this is Mark Johnson aboard the Cagliostro. Your command and control ship is destroyed. You are ordered to surrender and prepare your ships to be boarded."

A moment passed with no reply, then a voice crackled over the communications unit.

"We will still destroy your entire fleet and then rain death on what is left of your world."

Instantly the Agalum ships that were able to, began to line up as the dual prongs on each ship's bow extended and began to glow.

"I seen this show before," Dan growled. "I hope you got a trick up yer sleeve fer this one." The powerhouse pilot/engineer turned towards Mark hopefully.

On the main view screen before them, the remainder of the earth fleet continued to bombard their enemies relentlessly.

"They're not even firing back on our ships anymore." Eddie commented as he turned toward Mark, "You better hurry boss, I think this is the final round and these guys are going for the knockout."

Mark was staring at his display as he punched buttons and entered figures into a virtual pad that was suspended over the desk on his command chair.

"Boss, hurry!" Danny implored.

"Working on it," Mark replied quietly, as he concentrated.

"Not to put too much pressure on you boss, but now would be good," Red added.

"Working…"

Eddie turned nervously and looked at Mark, "Boss, you gotta hurry, if these guys fire that thing again, every earth ship will be destroyed, or de-powered. If this line of defense goes down, the planets a goner!"

In space the prongs on each of the enemy ships glowed brighter and then energy began to arc across their bows, connecting one ship to another.

"Dan, check this quick." a display opened above Dan's desk showing the mathematics Mark was working on.

Dan wasted no time, nodding his approval almost immediately. "Looks good."

"Eddie, fire!" Mark ordered.

Eddie found a button glowing on his console and his aiming reticle was already up and ready. He didn't hesitate at all as he aimed and fired in one precise motion, instantly a beam of energy streamed from the ships forward weapons array, directly at the energy stream that was now arcing through space connecting the Agalum ships. The ray from the Cagliostro interrupted the arcing energy as it reached between the Agalum vessels and suddenly, spectacularly the enemy ships connected by the arcing stream shuddered for a nano-second before simultaneously exploding brightly, spraying near space with untold tons of debris from the enemy ships, which had exploded one after another straight down a many miles long line.

"Wow," Eddie DiGenovese almost whispered.

"Yeah Eddie, that just about sums it all up." Mark replied stoically as he flopped back into his chair and watched the small particles begin to burn up in Earth's atmosphere, leaving small fiery trails towards the planet's surface, but disappearing as they turned to ash long before they would ever reach it.

The command crew continued to stare at Mark with a combination of relief and shock upon their faces.

Mark saw this and continued,

"What? You guys were actually worried? We had eleven seconds, I measured the time it took to fire that thing from the last time they used it at the asteroid belt."

"And how long did that take?" Eddie asked.

Mark grinned, "Ten point two, we had plenty of time."

Chapter Twenty Nine

The fighting was not over yet. For two more days above Earth's surface, as well as upon it, the battles raged. In space, Earth's fleet, as well as her space stations harangued the remnants of the enemy fleet. Taking whole ships captive and destroying others. Mark Johnson and the Cagliostro led and coordinated those efforts, driving the enemy away, or decimating them where they tried to make a stand.

Earth's fleet was now less than half of the size it had been, ship repair and reconstruction would commence immediately. The remaining ships would be placed in close proximity to Earth and her artificial satellites where ship building would be taking place.

On the evening of the second day a message was received from deep space. The president immediately contacted Mark Johnson and spoke to him behind closed doors.

Mark exited his conference room, rubbing his chin in thought as he sat down in his command chair. Ariel noticed the look on his face, and then nudged him mentally.

'*What is it?*' Her mental voice rode through his mind.

He looked at her and answered through their psychic link. '*We just received a threat from the Agalum high command. Basically a 'This is not over, we'll be back.' type of message.*'

'*So why'd President Scaleia want to speak to you about it?*'

'*He figures I have as much of a stake in this battle as anyone else planet-side. He even offered me the opportunity to respond to our 'friends' out there.*'

'*Are you going to?*' Her mental voice sang across his mind.

'*Yes. I'm just trying to figure out what to say.*'

'*How about 'Don't bother, we're coming for you.'?*'

'*I sometimes forget what I find attractive about you. Besides the obvious, I mean.*' He smiled, lasciviously.

'*And here I thought it was just my looks all along.*' She returned his smile.

'*Well, that too,*' he shrugged and winked.

"Will you two cut it out?" Dan Sledge interrupted, "Everyone here can see you're having one o' your psychic conversations again. At least clue the rest of us in on what's goin' on."

Ariel stood up, walked two seats down from her post to Dan's and kissed him on the cheek , then said "We were just commenting on how cute you were behind your little desk."

The big Jovian turned red, then smirked, "Get outta here Ari," and laughed as she took her seat again.

Mark sat back as the chuckles on his command deck died down about him. The tension was beginning to ease from everyone after the past few days and weeks of hell. Starships of both fleets lay about earth's orbit, floating in haphazard positions, with energy trails sputtering out of ruined power cores. Many more just floated in place, dead. The destroyed enemy ships would be hauled off to Mars where they could be dissected and melted down, their metals made ready for re-use as part of new ships that needed to be built to replace destroyed ones. Captured and functional enemy ships would be taken apart and put back together, replacing key systems with Earthly components, and then those ships would also be made part of the new fleet.

"Ari," Mark began, "get ready to record a message for our newfound friends out there."

She nodded indicating she was ready. Mark stood and faced where he knew the command deck camera was placed and began to speak. "To the Agalum race, if that is really what you call yourselves, this is Captain Mark Johnson of the Earth Protectorate Interstellar Command, hereafter known as 'EPIC'. As of now you are on notice. You claimed that we were seen as a threat to you and your interests in deep space, and yet you live and exist almost a week away from Earth at top hyper-warp speed. You claim that you fear our weaponry, and our so called savagery, and yet you attacked us, seeking to exterminate or separate all life upon our world and scatter it across the universe. You infiltrated our society at the highest levels of government, replacing our highest ranking leaders on God only knows how many fronts and sought to destroy us from within. You kidnapped and tortured those selfsame individuals as well as members of my crew. Then, you committed an even higher crime against my entire world. You sought to raze it out from under us while we watched.

But that was your last mistake. Your first was getting involved with us at all. You should have greeted us with open arms and palms up, welcoming us, as part of the greater universe. Instead, you sought to destroy us supposedly based on your own fears."

"The problem with your reasoning is you did not act as a fearful people. You acted as conquerors and tyrants. Tyrants always hide behind words like 'We know what's best' and 'Disarm potential threats'. You don't understand, or perhaps you didn't look deep enough to realize, that we, as a race, have a history of dealing with tyrants and conquerors. A very definitive history."

Mark walked across the command deck as he continued to speak, "So you may ask yourself what am I getting at here, and why am I taking so long to get to the point? Well that's a reasonable set of questions and I'm going to indulge you on those questions. The reason I haven't gotten to the point is that, well, let me put it this way, on my world there's a couple of old sayings that really bear paying heed to, especially by you and right now at this time and place. One is 'Let Sleeping Dragons Lie.' The other is 'Sow the wind, reap the whirlwind.' I'm not going to wait for you to figure out what either of those sayings means. The bottom line is, we're coming for you."

Definitely NOT
The End

www.ingramcontent.com/pod-product-compliance
Lightning Source LLC
Chambersburg PA
CBHW030115180626
46812CB00002B/432